11-05-2006

Dear Jane,

 We hope you enjoy
This book. We miss you,
and hope you are well.
 Happy Thanksgiving.

Love,
Gordon

# THE SEASONS OF THE SWANS

# THE SEASONS OF THE SWANS

## F. GORDON FOSTER, M.D.

Printed in the United States of America.

ISBN-13:  978-0-9760563-3-1
ISBN-10:  0-9760563-3-X
Library of Congress Control Number:  2005935178

**MECHLING** BOOKBINDERY

1124 Oneida Valley Road - Rt. 38
Chicora, PA 16025-3820
www.mechlingbooks.com

To my family

# ACKNOWLEDGEMENTS

This book would not have been possible without the contribution made by Emilie Tucker. She not only provided the technical skills that I lack, but she shared my enthusiasm every moment, every page along the way.

I would also like to thank Rebecca Brown and Nancy Gresko, reference librarians at Butler Area Public Library in Butler Pennsylvania. Over the course of two years they found specific poems that now illustrate this book.

I am grateful to Kari McConnell, whose photographic and publishing expertise organized the visual presentation in it's final form.

# TABLE OF CONTENTS

PROLOGUE

Nathan, Leonard:  Diary of a Left-Handed Birdwatcher

WINTER

Rexroth, Kenneth:  *The Collected Longer Poems of Kenneth Rexroth*, "Leda Hidden".                                        2
Wilbur, Richard:  *Ceremony And Other Poems*, "Year's End".                                                              4
Emerson, Ralph Waldo:  *The Complete Poems of Ralph Waldo Emerson*, "The Snow-Storm".                                    6
Succop, Margaret Phillips:  *Climb To The Stars*, "A Winter Day".                                                        8
Wylie, Elinor:  *The Collected Poems of Elinor Wylie*, "Velvet Shoes".                                                   9
Clief-Stefanon, Lyrae Van:  *Black Swan*, "Leda".                                                                        10
Rilke, Rainer Maria:  *New Poems [1908]: The Other Part*, " Leda", translated by Edward Snow.                            12
Bogan, Louise:  *The Blue Estuaries*, "Winter Swan".                                                                     14
Eliot, T.S.:  *The Quartets*, "Little Gidding".                                                                          16
Hollander, John:  *Selected Poetry*, "Metathalamia".                                                                     18
Randall, Jarrell:  *The Complete Poems*, "The Black Swan".                                                               20
Mallarmé, Stéphane:  *The Anchor Anthology of French Poetry from Nerval to Valery*,
                "The Pristine, The Perennial, and the Beauteous Today…", translated by Katie Flores.                    25
Yeats, W.B.:  *The Collected Works of W.B. Yeats*, "Leda and the Swan".                                                  26
Horan, Robert:  *The Yale Younger Poets Anthology*, "Soft Swimmer, Winter Swan".                                         28
Sarton, May:  *The Silence Now and New and Uncollected Earlier Poems*, "Blizzard".                                      30
Larkin, Philip:  *Collected Poems*, "Blizzard".                                                                          30
Larkin, Philip:  *Collected Poems,* "Winter".                                                                           36
Dickey, James:  *Poems (1959 – 1967)*, "Fog Envelopes the Animals".                                                     38
Jeffers, Robinson:  *The Collected Poetry of Robinson Jeffers*, "Flight of Swan".                                       40
MacEwen, Gwendolyn:  *Afterworlds*, "The Death of the Loch Ness Monster".                                               42
Lawrence, D.H.:  *The Plumed Serpent*, "The Living Quetzalcoatl".                                                        44
Meredith, William:  *Effort at Speech: New and Selected Poems*, "Orpheus".                                              46
Vinal, Harold:  *The Yale Younger Poets Anthology*, "To Persephone".                                                     48

Roethke, Theodore: *The Collected Poems of Theodore Roethke*, "The Swan".     50

Plath, Sylvia: *The Collected Poems*, "Winter Landscape, with Rooks".     52

H.D. (Doolittle, Hilda): *Collected Poems 1912 – 1944*, "Birds in Snow".     54

## Spring

Thomas, Dylan: *The Poems of Dylan Thomas*, "The Force That Through The Green Fuse Drives The Flower".     58

Chaucer, Geoffrey: *The Canterbury Tales*, "The Prologe".     60

Eliot, T.S.: *Collected Poems 1909 – 1962*, "The Waste Land, I. The Burial of the Dead".     60

Fallon, Peter: *Contemporary Irish Poetry: An Anthology*, "Spring Song".     62

Barber, Theodore Xenophon: *The Human Nature of Birds*, "Flexible Territoriality".     64

Spenser, Edmund: *The New Oxford Book of Sixteenth Century Verse*, "Prothalamion".     66

Porter, Anne: *An Altogether Different Language: Poems 1934 – 1994*, "An Easter Lily".     68

White, E.B.: *The Trumpet of the Swan*, "A Visitor".     69

Moore, Marianne: *The Complete Poems of Marianne Moore*, "No Swan So Fine".     83

Kunitz, Stanley: *The Collected Poems*, "When The Light Falls".     84

Coatsworth, Elizabeth: *Poems (1957)*, "The Swan".     88

Shakespeare, William: *King John, Act V, Scene VII 4 – 50*, "Cygnet to this pale faint swan".     89

Lorenz, Konrad Z.: *King Solomon's Ring (1952)*, "The Perennial Retainers".     90

The Holy Bible: *King James Version*, "The Song of Solomon", Chapter 2, 1 – 13.     92

Longley, Michael: *Selected Poems*, "Swans Mating".     94

Clief-Stefanon, Lyrae Van: *Black Swan*, "Black Swan".     96

Wilbur, Richard: *Walking to Sleep: New Poems and Translations*, "Under Cygnus".     100

The Holy Bible: *King James Version*, "Leviathan" (Isaiah 27:1, Psalm 104:26, Job 41:1-2).     106

## Summer

Thomas, Dylan: *Collected Poems 1934 – 1952*, "Fern Hill".     110

Neruda, Pablo: *Extravagaria*, "Pastoral", translated by Alastair Reid.     112

Dickinson, Emily: *The Poems of Emily Dickinson*, "Hope Is The Thing With Feathers".     114

Tennyson, Alfred Lord: *A Collection of Poems*, "The Dragonfly" from The Two Voices.     115

Merrill, James: *Collected Poems*, "To   A Butterfly".     116

Merrill, James: *Collected Poems,* "The Black Swan".     118

Apollinaire, Guillaume: *The Anchor Anthology of French Poetry from Nerval to Valery*, "Dusk", Dudley Fitts.     124

Gershwin, George; Gershwin, Ira; Heyward, Dubose and Dorothy, *Porgy and Bess,* "Summertime".     126

McNeill, Louise:  *Hill Daughter:  New and Selected Poems (1991)*, "Memoria".    127

Niklander, Hannu:  *Nicely Curtsying Daughter*, "The Swan".    128

Nash, Ogden:  *The New Yorker 1950*, "The Swan."    129

*The Kabir Book*, "The Swan", translated by Robert Bly.    130

Rilke, Rainer Maria:  *Selected Poems*, "The Swan", translated by Albert Ernest Fleming.    132

Lawrence, D.H.:  *The Complete Poems of D.H. Lawrence*, "Leda".    132

Anderson, Maggie:  *A Space Filled With Moving*, "Summer Solstice".    134

Baudelaire, Charles:  *Halfway Down the Hall, New and Selected Poems*, "The Swan", translated by Rachel Hadas.    136

Coleridge, Samuel Taylor:  "The Desired Swan-Song".    138

Lawrence, D.H.:  *The Complete Poems of D. H. Lawrence*, "Swan".    139

Lucie-Smith, Edward:  *Voices in the Gallery*, "Blue".    140

# Fall

Auden, Wystan Hugh:  *On this Island*, "Now The Leaves Are Falling Fast".    144

Succop, Margaret Phillips:  *Climb to the Stars*, "Autumn Leaves".    146

Hopkins, Gerard Manley:  *The Poems of Gerard Manley Hopkins by Hopkins*, "Spring and Fall".    147

Merrill, James:  *Collected Poems* ,"Thistledown".    148

Zabel, Morton Dauwen:  *Poetry*, "Hoar Frost".    150

Merwin, W.S.:  *Flower and Hand: Poems 1977 – 1983*, "Autumn Evening".    152

Hölderlin, Friedrich:  *Hymns and Fragment*, "Half of Life".    153

MacLeish, Archibald:  *Collected Poems (1917 – 1982)*, "Immortal Autumn".    154

Carruth, Hayden:  *Collected Shorter Poems, 1946 – 1991*, "The Wild Swans at Norfolk".    156

Tennyson, Alfred Lord:  *A Collection of Poems*, "The Dying Swan".    158

Bierlein, J.F.:  *Parallel Myths*, "Angus Og".    160

Gibbons, Orlando:  *The First Set of Madrigals and Mottet of 5*, "The Silver Swanne".    162

Aesop Fables:  "The Swan and Goose", translated by William Ellery Leonard.    162

Yeats, W.B.:  *The Collected Works of W.B. Yeats*, "The Wild Swans at Coole".    164

Baring-Gould, Sabine:  *Myths of the Middle Ages*, "Swan-Maidens Pg. 120".    166

Frazer, Sir James George:  *The Golden Bough:  A Study in Magic and Religion*, "The External Soul in Folk Tales".    168

Helprin, Mark:  *Swan Lake*, "Pg 48 lines 6 – 12".    170

Baring-Gould, Sabine:  *Myths of the Middle Ages*, "Swan-Maidens Pg 116".    172

Guerber, H.A.:  *Myths Of The Norsemen:  From the Eddas and Sagas*, "Wayland and the Valkyrs", translated by Thorpe.    174

Eschenbach, Wolfram Von:  *"Parzival"* translated by A.T. Hatto 1980.    176

Southey, Robert:  *Poems of Robert Southey:*  Ballads and Metrical Tales, "Rudiger".    178

Lindsay, Vachel:  *Johnny Appleseed and Other Poems*, "On The Garden Wall".                    180
Poe, Edgar Allan:  *Tamerlane and Other Poems*, "Fanny".                                         181
Meredith, William:  *Effort At Speech*, "Poem".                                                 182
Oliver, Mary:  *No Voyage and Other Poems*, "Swans on the River Ayr".                            184
Hollander, John:  *Types of Shape*, "Swan and Shadow".                                          186

EPILOGUE
    Rexroth, Kenneth:  *The Selected Longer Poems*, "The Silver Swan II".                        188

BIBLIOGRAPHY                                                                                     189

GLOSSARY                                                                                         197

APPENDIX                                                                                         200

INDEX                                                                                            202

# INTRODUCTION

Born in 1943, Gordon Foster, M.D., decided at age four that he wanted to be a doctor. He never strayed from that path. After medical school, he spent time at UCLA, Yale, the U.S. Army Corps, and The University of Pittsburgh, before settling down for twenty-five years at Butler Hospital. Three years ago, however, he suffered a massive stroke. It left him with foreign accent syndrome and fluent aphasia. Dr. Foster stood at a crossroads. If he did nothing, then his mood, cognition, and social functions would continue to deteriorate. He, however, decided that he would do all he could do to overcome his condition. Therein lies the genesis of this book.

He had originally planned to compose a book of photographs about swans when he reached the age of seventy-five. Instead, at age fifty-nine, he decided that writing the book would be a good way to battle fluent aphasia. The book had been, for some twenty years, a labor of love. During that time, he had taken more than twenty thousand photographs and kept meticulous charts, graphs, and other scientific records—all amounting to a comprehensive natural history the likes of which we rarely find today. Writing the book became more than rehabilitation; it was also a means of regaining a lease on life. He decided to take up challenges he might not have ever taken up before: learning to use a computer, conducting lengthy research expeditions in the library, and the many other tasks involved in writing a book.

Let me now provide some background information that might help you appreciate the kind of book Gordon has written. It all relates to his decision to present poetry and pictures together. From as early as antiquity, there has always been a fruitful and inspiring relationship between painting and poetry, the visual arts and the verbal arts. That relationship is encapsulated in the phrase *ut pictura poesis*: poems are speaking pictures; pictures are mute poems. Over the years we have seen poetry and pictures correlated when, for example, paintings have inspired poems and poems have inspired paintings. We have also seen the relationship between pictures and poems in such places as emblem books, which were read to tatters for centuries. In an emblem book, the author wishes to illustrate an idea, such as the nature of peace. To do so, he avails himself of two facing pages. On one page, he writes out that which he wishes to state about, say, peace. On the facing page, he offers a picture depicting peace. Together, the picture and the poem should impact the reader with a synesthetic message.

Now we see the way that Dr. Foster continues this artistic tradition by juxtaposing passages of poetry with pictures of swans. He has united the best of both worlds. The swan is the most elegant and majestic of birds, and the poem is the most lofty discourse among discourses. From both, he has chosen his favorites. From twenty thousand photographs of swans, he selected the one hundred he cherishes the most. Similarly, he includes here his favorite poems, the ones that had resonated in his imagination for years, if not decades. Indeed, this book springs from many, many years of preparation and cultivation.  It reflects his beautiful mind.

The pictures are all the more beautiful for being taken at his lovely rural home, which is an Audubon Sanctuary.  Its landscape is characterized by the same topography which characterizes western Pennsylvania:  rolling hills, forests, ponds, and wetlands.  One could easily imagine Henry David Thoreau spending a year beside Gordon Foster's pond, enjoying its landscape, observing its swans, and quietly meditating upon all that this pastoral setting evokes.  One could also envision Robert Frost pausing to gaze upon the pond and its environs as he trudged home late one evening.

All in all, Gordon's book is meant to be savored, like a glass of fine wine.  It is meant to be read slowly, to be enjoyed with the same enjoyment that he invested in it.  Place it on your coffee table. When you pick it up and encounter the picture and poem, reflect upon the two together, for they are conceived as one.  If you allow the book to speak to you, then you will receive from it what Gordon wishes for you to receive:  an appreciation of beauty, an exposure to timeless poetry, an education in waterfowl, a feeling of peace, and a blessing upon your heart and soul.

Michael W. Price, PhD
30 October 2005

# PROLOGUE

---

I point out to him that poetry and birds have been associated from the beginning of civilization, probably before. I remind him that ancient poets put birds into their poems not just as symbols for human feelings but also as authentic forms of otherness. Sappho, when she wants to represent Aphrodite, the Goddess of Love, in her chariot, has it drawn not by horses, the tame servants of humans, but by wild birds, "beautiful swift sparrows" with a whir of "fast-beating wings." Birds appear in poems to show states of mind that go beyond the human. Horace, in one of his odes, imagines himself transformed at his death into a great bird, "the rough skin already" gathering on his legs. This transformation complete, he will soar above the world and death to become a wonder to those gazing up into the heavens from every quarter of the globe. Birds enter poems to mediate between us and the world.

Leonard
Nathan

# WINTER

# LEDA HIDDEN

Christmas Eve, unseasonably cold,
I walk in Golden Gate Park.
The winter twilight thickens.
The park grows dusky before
The usual hour.  The sky
Sinks close to the shadowy
Trees, and sky and trees mingle
In receding planes of vagueness.
The wet pebbles on the path
Wear little frills of ice like
Minute, transparent fungus.
Suddenly the air is full
Of snowflakes – cold, white, downy
Feathers that do not seem to
Come from the sky but crystallize
Out of the air.  The snow is
Unendurably beautiful,
Falling in the breathless lake,
Floating in the yellow rushes.
I cannot feel the motion
Of the air, but it makes a sound
In the rushes, and the snow
Falling through their weaving blades
Makes another sound. I stand still,
Breathing as gently as I can,

And listen to those two sounds,
And watch the web of frail wavering
Motion until it is almost night.
I walk back along the lake path
Pure white with the new snow.  Far out
Into the dusk the unmoving
Water is drinking the snow.
Out of the thicket of winter
Cattails, almost at my feet,
Thundering and stamping his wings,
A huge white swan plunges away.
He breaks out of the tangle,
And floats suspended on gloom.
Only his invisible
Black feet move in the cold water.
He floats away into the dark,
Until he is a white blur
Like a face lost in the night,
And then he is gone. All the world
Is quiet and motionless
Except for the fall and whisper
Of snow.  There is nothing but night,
And the snow and the odor
Of the frosty water.

Kenneth Rexroth

2

# YEAR'S END

Now winter downs the dying of the year,
And night is all a settlement of snow;
From the soft street the rooms of houses show
A gathered light, a shapen atmosphere,
Like frozen-over lakes whose ice is thin
And still allows some stirring down within.

I've known the wind by water banks to shake
The late leaves down, which frozen where they fell
And held in ice as dancers in a spell
Fluttered all winter long into a lake;
Graved on the dark in gestures of descent,
They seemed their own most perfect monument.

There was perfection in the death of ferns
Which laid their fragile cheeks against the stone
A million years. Great mammoths overthrown
Composedly have made their long sojourns,
Like palaces of patience, in the gray
And changeless lands of ice. And at Pompeii

The little dog lay curled and did not rise
But slept the deeper as the ashes rose

And found the people incomplete, and froze
The random hands, the loose unready eyes
Of men expecting yet another sun
To do the shapely thing they had not done.

These sudden ends of time must give us pause.
We fray into the future, rarely wrought
Save in the tapestries of afterthought.
More time, more time. Barrages of applause
Come muffled from a buried radio.
The New-year bells are wrangling with the snow.

Richard Wilbur

# THE SNOWSTORM

Announced by all the trumpets of the sky,
Arrives the snow, and, driving o'er the fields,
Seems nowhere to alight:  the whited air
Hides hills and woods, the river, and the heaven,
And veils the farmhouse at the garden's end.
The sled and traveler stopped, the courier's feet
Delayed, all friends shut out, the housemates sit
Around the radiant fireplace, inclosed
In a tumultuous privacy of storm.

Come, see the north wind's masonry.
Out of an unseen quarry evermore
Furnished with tile, the fierce artificer
Curves his white bastions with projected roof
Round every windward stake, or tree, or door.
Speeding, the myriad-handed, his wild work
So fanciful, so savage, naught cares he
For number or proportion.  Mockingly
On coop or kennel he hangs Parian wreaths;
A swan-like form invests the hidden thorn;
Fills up the farmer's lane from wall to wall,
Maugre the farmer's sighs; and at the gate
A tapering turret overtops the work.
And when his hours are numbered, and the world
Is all his own, retiring, as he were not,
Leaves, when the sun appears, astonished Art
To mimic in slow structures, stone by stone,
Built in an age, the mad wind's night-work,
The frolic architecture of the snow.

Ralph Waldo Emerson

# A WINTER DAY

The hills and valleys are covered with snow,
Brushed with crystals of ice that glow
From towering trees, from shrubs, each tiny strand
Glistens in winter's fairyland.
The snow, like a veil, drawn across earth's face,
Falls from each branch like frothy lace.
And the wind fingers lightly hill and plain,
Chanting a soft cathedral strain.
Through the windowed trees, the sun's clear bright
gaze
Cloaks the world in a golden haze,
Transforming this earthly vision of ice
To reflection of Paradise.

Margaret Phillips Succop

# Velvet Shoes

Let us walk in the white snow
In a soundless space;
With footsteps quiet and slow,
At a tranquil pace,
Under veils of white lace.

I shall go shod in silk,
And you in wool,
White as a white cow's milk,
More beautiful
Than the breast of a gull.

We shall walk through the still town
In a windless peace;
We shall step upon white down,
Upon silver fleece,
Upon softer than these.

We shall walk in velvet shoes:
Wherever we go
Silence will fall like dews
On white silence below.
We shall walk in the snow.

Elinor Wylie

# LEDA

*For my mother*

Imagine Leda black —
skinny legs     peach-switch
scarred     vaselined to gleaming
like magnolia leaves   Imagine
a teenager     hips asway like moss
switchin' down a dirt road
Florida orange blossom
water behind her ears
her tight sheath-skirt
azalea pink
A freemason Pentecostal
preacher's child
sent down from the city
to be raised by her grandmama
A girl     assured her whole like
I *never asked for you no-how!*
I *asked for your sister.*
Imagine
the god/swan's neck
draped around her neck
like a white down noose
For years she walked straight
Home from school     past tempting
crescent lakes     warned off
from sweet patches
of sugarcane
because of the snakes
and the gators

Lyrae Van Clief-Stefanon

# LEDA

When the god in his great need crossed inside,
he was shocked almost to find the swan so beautiful;
he slipped himself inside it all confused.
But his deceit bore him toward the deed

before he'd put that untried being's
feelings to the test.  And the opened woman
saw at once who was coming in the swan
and understood:  he asked *one* thing

which she, confused in her resistance,
no longer could hold back.  The god came down
and necking through the ever weaker hand

released himself into the one he loved.
Then only – with what delight! – he felt his feathers
and grew truly swan within her womb.

Rainer Maria Rilke

# WINTER SWAN

It is a hollow garden, under the cloud;
Beneath the heel a hollow earth is turned;
Within the mind the live blood shouts aloud;
Under the breast the willing blood is burned,
Shut with the fire passed and the fire returned.
But speak, you proud!
Where lies the leaf-caught world once thought abiding,
Now but a dry disarray and artifice?
Here, to the ripple cut by the cold, drifts this
Bird, the long throat bent back, and the eyes in hiding.

Louise Bogan

PEN AND COB BUILDING THEIR WINTER NEST.

# LITTLE GIDDING

Midwinter spring is its own season
Sempiternal though sodden towards sundown,
Suspended in time, between pole and tropic.
When the short day is brightest, with frost and fire,
The brief sun flames the ice, on pond and ditches,
In windless cold that is the heart's heat,
Reflecting in a watery mirror
A glare that is blindness in the early afternoon.
And glow more intense than blaze of branch, or brazier,
Stirs the dumb spirit:  no wind, but pentecostal fire
In the dark time of the year.  Between melting and freezing
The soul's sap quivers.  There is no earth smell
Or smell of living thing.  This is the spring time
But not in time's covenant.  Now the hedgerow
Is blanched for an hour with transitory blossom
Of snow, a bloom more sudden
Than that of summer, neither budding nor fading,
Not in the scheme of generation.
Where is the summer, the unimaginable
Zero summer?

T.S. Eliot

# METATHALAMIA

After the midwinter marriages—the bride of snow
Now of one body with the black ground, the ice-heiress
Bedded with her constant rock, the far hills of one mind
With the bare sky now, and the emperor of rivers
Joined with the most recent of his flowing concubines—
After the choirs of the cold have died on the late air,
Low now as our unagitated humdrum heartbeats
Still go about their irreversible chores again,
You and I have heard the song of the long afterword:
The phrases of the moon crooning to the fields below,
The cracking language of frozen forests whose summer
Harps were long since smashed, and the profound, recurrent vow
This bright stream's soft echoing answer rings to the woods.

John Hollander

# THE BLACK SWAN

When the swans turned my sister into a swan
I would go to the lake, at night, from milking:
The sun would look out through the reeds like a swan,
A swan's red beak; and the beak would open
And inside there was darkness, the stars and the moon.

Out on the lake a girl would laugh.
"Sister, here is your porridge, sister,"
I would call; and the reeds would whisper,
"Go to sleep, go to sleep, little swan."
My legs were all hard and webbed, and the silky

Hairs of my wings sank away like stars
In the ripples that ran in and out of the reeds:
I heard through the lap and hiss of water
Someone's "Sister ... sister," far away on the shore,
And then as I opened my beak to answer

I heard my harsh laugh go out to the shore
And saw – saw at last, swimming up from the green
Low mounds of the lake, the white stone swans:
The white, named swans ... "It is all a dream,"
I whispered, and reached from the down of the pallet

To the lap and hiss of the floor.
And "Sleep, little sister," the swans all sang
From the moon and stars and frogs of the floor.
But the swan my sister called, "Sleep at last, little sister,"
And stroked all night, with a black wing, my wings.

Randall Jarrell

PEN INCUBATING HER NEST

PEN WITH TWO CYGNETS…RIME WARMS WINTER'S SUN.

Black Australian swans bring algae to the surface for the cygnets.

Winter Twilight

# THE PRISTINE, THE PERENNIAL AND THE BEAUTEOUS TODAY...

*Le vierge, le vivace et le bel aujourd'hui...*

The pristine, the perennial, the beauteous today,
May it crack for us with lunge of drunken wing
This hard, forsaken lake haunted beneath its crust
By the crystalline ice of flights not ever flown!

— A quondam swan recalls that it is he,
Magnificent but in despair of extricating himself,
Having left unsung the region where to be
When winter glistened sterile with ennui.

All his neck will be disburdened of this white agony
Imposed by space upon the bird denying it,
But not of his loathing of the ground where trapped his
plumage lies.

Phantasm to this place consigned by his utter grandeur,
He immures himself in the frigid dream of scorn
Which in his fruitless exile swathes the Swan.

Stéphane Mallarmé
Translated by Kate Flores

# LEDA AND THE SWAN

A sudden blow:  the great wings beating still
Above the staggering girl, her thighs caressed
By the dark webs, her nape caught in his bill,
He holds her helpless breast upon his breast.

How can those terrified vague fingers push
The feathered glory from her loosening thighs?
And how can body, laid in that white rush,
But feel the strange heart beating where it lies?

A shudder in the loins engenders there
The broken wall, the burning roof and tower
And Agamemnon dead.
                        Being so caught up
So mastered by the brute blood of the air,
Did she put on his knowledge with his power
Before the indifferent beak could let her drop?

W. B. Yeats

# SOFT SWIMMER, WINTER SWAN

The sun shows thin through hail, wallpaper-pale, and falls
grey from its royal world toward colder poles.
Gone, like a grave swan gone blossoming in bone,
a white tree of feathers, blown singly down.

A last, a light, and caught in the air-ladder lark,
south-driven, climbing the indian, swift dark, and listen!
Sped by the building cold and rare in ether, birds hasten
the heart already taxed with cloud and cherubim –
fretted heaven, strained songless and flown dim.
Out from the house that held them in safe summer,
small ponds and blue counties, the chequered swimmers
in air, spring sudden through the closing vault of frost.
(The last, awakened by a late storm, are forever lost.)

But the calm swan, adamant in autumn, passes
through still willowed water, parting the yellow rushes.
His eye, like a lighted nail, sees the vast
distance of amethyst roll under him, the marble beast.

Seen from the shore, this bird but luminous boat,
so motionless in speed, quiet, will float
forward in cold time, disdaining harbor; marooned
in infinite roads of rivers, his wings wrought around
to muffle danger and battle with the wind;
safe, slow, calm, a ship with frail lights, a white swan.

But seen from beneath, the soft statue hardens; the wild feet
must wrest from this pure prison some retreat,
outdistance winter and oblivion; now, in feverish motion, foam
the careless waters, throat, wing, heart, all spotless in arched bone.

Pressed, must push farther on through lakes where winter lies
secret and dumb in shallows, building bright fields of ice
to trap the transparent fish, turn the wet world to stone,
surprise the soft swimmer and capture the winter swan.

We see, serene, this desperate passage through perfect seas;
taught to see ease in agony, see only ease.
In the battle of snow against snow and wind upon wind
the dead lie fooled in the ice, too far to find.

Robert Horan

# BLIZZARD

Hard to imagine daffodils
Where I see nothing but white veils
Incessant falling of thick snow
In this nowhere, non-landscape
Which has no shadow and no shape,
And holds me fast and holds me deep
And will not cease before I sleep.
Hard to imagine somewhere else
Where life could stir and has a pulse,
And know that somewhere else will be
This very field, changed utterly,
With hosts of daffodils to show
That spring was there under the snow.
New Englanders are skeptical
Of what cannot depend on will,
Yet I should know that this wide range
Of white and green and constant change
Have kept me kindled, on the edge of fear,
Travelling the weather like a mountaineer.

May Sarton

# BLIZZARD

Suddenly clouds of snow
Begin assaulting the air,
As falling, as tangled
As a girl's thick hair.

Some see a flock of swans,
Some a fleet of ships
Or a spread winding-sheet,
But the snow touches my lips

And beyond all doubt I know
A girl is standing there
Who will take no lovers
Till she winds me in her hair.

Philip Larkin

SILENCE

Serenity

SUNDIAL AT 0900

WIND

# WINTER

In the field, two horses,
Two swans on the river,
While a wind blows over
A waste of thistles
Crowded like men;
And now again
My thoughts are children
With uneasy faces
That awake and rise
Beneath running skies
From buried places.

For the line of a swan
Diagonal on water
Is the cold of winter,
And each horse like a passion
Long since defeated
Lowers its head,
And oh, they invade
My cloaked-up mind
Till memory unlooses
Its brooch of faces –
Streams far behind.

Then the whole heath whistles
In the leaping wind,
And shrivelled men stand
Crowding like thistles
To one fruitless place;
Yet still the miracles
Exhume in each face
Strong silken seed,
That to the static
Gold winter sun throws back.
Endless and cloudless pride.

Philip Larkin

# FOG ENVELOPS THE ANIMALS

Fog envelops the animals.
Not one can be seen, and they live.
At my knees, a cloud wears slowly
Up out of the buried earth.
In a white suit I stand waiting.

Soundlessly whiteness is eating
My visible self alive.
I shall enter this world like the dead,
Floating through tree trunks on currents
And streams of untouchable pureness

That shine without thinking of light.
My hands burn away at my sides
In the pale, risen ghosts of deep river.
In my hood peaked like a flame,
I feel my own long-hidden,

Long-sought invisibility

Come forth from my solid body.
I stand with all beasts in a cloud.
Of them I am deadly aware,
And they not of me, in this life.
Only my front teeth are showing
As the dry fog mounts to my lips
In a motion long buried in water,
And now, one by one, my teeth
Like rows of candles go out.

In the spirit of flame, my hood
Holds the face of my soul without burning,
And I drift forward
Through the hearts of the curdling oak trees,
Borne by the river of Heaven.

My arrows, keener than snowflakes,
Are with me whenever I touch them.
Above my head, the trees exchange their arms
In the purest fear upon earth.
Silence. Whiteness. Hunting.

James Dickey

# FLIGHT OF SWANS

One who sees giant Orion, the torches of winter midnight,
Enormously walking above the ocean in the west of heaven;
And watches the track of this age of time at its peak of flight
Waver like a spent rocket, wavering toward new discoveries,
Mortal examinations of darkness, soundings of depth;
And watches the long coast mountain vibrate from bronze to green,
Bronze to green, year after year, and all the streams;
Dry and flooded, dry and flooded, in the racing seasons;
And knows that exactly this and not another is the world,
The ideal is phantoms for bait, the spirit is a flicker on a grave; -
May serve, with a certain detachment, the fugitive human race,
Or his own people, or his own household; but hardly himself;
And will not wind himself into hopes nor sicken with despairs.
He has found the peace and adored the God; he handles in autumn
The germs of far-future spring.

Sad sons of the stormy fall,
No escape, you have to inflict and endure:  surely it is time for you
To learn to touch the diamond within to the diamond outside,
Thinning your humanity a little between the invulnerable diamonds,
Knowing that your angry choices and hopes and terrors are in vain,
But life and death not in vain; and the world is like a flight of swans.

Robinson Jeffers

# THE DEATH OF THE LOCH NESS MONSTER

Consider that the thing has died before we proved it ever lived
and that it died of loneliness, dark lord of the loch,
fathomless Worm, great Orm, this last of our mysteries –
*haifend ane meikill fin on ilk syde*
*with ane taill and ane terribill heid* –
and that it had no tales to tell us, only that it lived there,
lake-locked, lost in its own coils,
waiting to be found; in the black light of midnight
surfacing, its whole elastic length unwound,
and the sound it made as it broke the water
was the single plucked string of a harp –
this newt or salamander, graceful as a swan,
this water-snake, this water-horse, this water-dancer.

Consider him tired of pondering the possible existence of man
whom he thinks he has sighted sometimes on the shore,
and rearing up from the purple churning water,
weird little worm head swaying from side to side,
he denies the vision before his eyes;
his long neck, swan of Hell, a silhouette against the moon,
his green heart beating its last,
his noble, sordid soul in ruins.

Now the mist is a blanket of doom, and we pluck from the depths
a prize of primordial slime –
the beast who was born from some terrible ancient kiss,
lovechild of unspeakable histories,
this ugly slug half blind no doubt, and very cold,
his head which is horror to behold
no bigger than our own;
whom we loathe, for his kind ruled the earth before us,
who died of loneliness in a small lake in Scotland,
and in his mind's dark land,
where he dreamed up his luminous myths, the last of which was man.

Gwendolyn MacEwen

# THE LIVING QUETZALCOATL

I am the Living Quetzalcoatl.
Naked I come from out of the deep
From the place which I call my Father.
Naked have I travelled the long way round
From heaven, past the sleeping sons of God.

Out of the depths of the sky, I came like an eagle.
Out of the bowels of the earth like a snake.

All things that lift in the lift of living between earth
    and sky, know me.

But I am the inward star invisible.
And the star is the lamp in the hand of the
    Unknown Mover.
Beyond me is a Lord who is terrible, and wonderful,
    and dark to me forever.
Yet I have lain in his loins, ere he begot me in
    Mother space.

Now I am alone on earth, and this is mine.
The roots are mine, down the dark, moist path of the snake.
And the branches are mine, in the paths of the sky
    and the bird,
But the spark of me that is me is more than mine own.

And the feet of men, and the hands of women
    know me.
And knees and thighs and loins, and the bowels of
    strength and seed are lit with me.
The snake of my left-hand out of the darkness is
    hissing your feet with his mouth of caressive fire,
And putting his strength in your heels and ankles, his
    flame in your knees and your legs and your loins,
    his circle of rest in your belly.
For I am Quetzalcoatl, the feathered snake,
And I am not with you till my serpent has coiled his
    circle of rest in your belly.
And I, Quetzalcoatl, the eagle of the air, am brushing
    your faces with vision.
I am fanning your breasts with my breath.
And building my nest of peace in your bones.
I am Quetzalcoatl, of the Two Ways.

D. H. Lawrence

Ice pearls

# ORPHEUS

The lute and my skill with it came unasked from Apollo,
But the girl I drew myself from the truck of a tree
And she lodged in me then as she had in the black willow.
I was tuned like strings: she had the skill of me.

She was taken by death on one of three pretenses:
A jealous brother, a jealous god, or a serpent.
The mind turns from causes in such cases –
All a man can say is, it happened.

Now with my father's favors, the lute and skill,
Through the dark smelly places where the gods play
With the unlucky, I ape a smiling way,
And do prodigious feats of vaudeville.

The meaningless ordeals I've tuned to meaning!
The foul caprice I've zithered into just!
As if my love were no more than a god's lust,
*Lend me Euridice,* I sing and sing.

William Meredith

# TO PERSEPHONE

No more you weave, Persephone,
Gowns the colors of the sea.

Your ivory fingers now are still
And your grave a grassy hill.

But everywhere songs are sung
They sing of you who died so young.

And lad and lassies passing by
Place bergamot where you lie.

No more you weave, Persephone,
Gowns the colors of the sea,

Emerald, chrysoprase and blue
That looked beautiful on you.

But everywhere songs are sung
They sing of you who died so young.

Harold Vinal

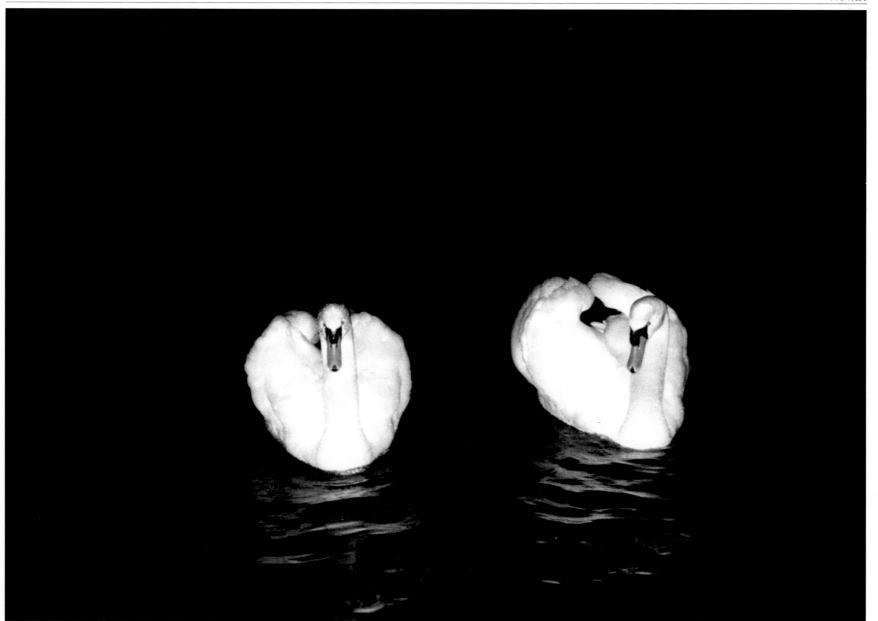

# THE SWAN

I study out a dark similitude:
Her image fades, yet does not disappear –
Must I stay tangled in that lively hair?
Is there no way out of that coursing blood?
A dry soul's wisest.  O, I am not dry!
My darling does what I could never do:
She sighs me white, a Socrates of snow.

We think too long in terms of what to be;
I live, alive and certain as a bull;
A casual man, I keep my casual word,
Yet whistle back at every whistling bird.
A man alive, from a light I must fall.
I am my father's son, I am John Donne
Whenever I see her with nothing on.

*The moon draws back its waters from the shore.*
*By the lake's edge, I see a silver swan,*
*And she is what I would.  In this light air,*
*Lost opposites bend down –*
*Sing of that nothing of which all is made,*
*Or listen into silence, like a god.*

Theodore Roethke

# WINTER LANDSCAPE, WITH ROOKS

Water in the millrace, through a sluice of stone,
plunges headlong into that black pond
where, absurd and out-of-season, a single swan
floats chaste as snow, taunting the clouded mind
which hungers to haul the white reflection down.

The austere sun descends above the fen,
an orange cyclops-eye, scorning to look
longer on this landscape of chagrin;
feathered dark in thought, I stalk like a rook,
brooding as the winter night comes on.

Last summer's reeds are all engraved in ice
as is your image in my eye; dry frost
glazes the window of my hurt; what solace
can be struck from rock to make heart's waste
grow green again?  Who'd walk in this bleak place?

Sylvia Plath

# BIRDS IN SNOW

See,
how they trace
across the very-marble
of this place,
bright sevens and printed fours,
elevens and careful eights,
abracadabra
of a mystic's lore
or symbol
outlined
on a wizard's gate;

like plaques of ancient writ
our garden flags now name
the great and very-great;
our garden flags acclaim
in carven hieroglyph,
here king and kinglet lie,
here prince and lady rest,
mystical queens sleep here
and heroes that are slain

in holy righteous war;
hieratic, slim and fair,
the tracery written here,
proclaims what's left unsaid
in Egypt of her dead.

H. D.

# SPRING

# THE FORCE THAT THROUGH THE GREEN FUSE DRIVES THE FLOWER

The force that through the green fuse drives the flower
Drives my green age; that blasts the roots of trees
Is my destroyer.
And I am dumb to tell the crooked rose
My youth is bent by the same wintry fever.

The force that drives the water through the rocks
Drives my red blood; that dries the mouthing streams
Turns mine to wax
And I am dumb to mouth unto my veins
How at the mountain spring the same mouth sucks.

The hand that whirls the water in the pool
Stirs the quicksand; that ropes the blowing wind
Hauls my shroud sail.
And I am dumb to tell the hanging man
How of my clay is made the hangman's lime.

The lips of time leech to the fountain head;
Love drips and gathers, but the fallen blood
Shall calm her sores.
And I am dumb to tell a weather's wind
How time has ticked a heaven round the stars.

And I am dumb to tell the lover's tomb
How at my sheet goes the same crooked worm.

Dylan Thomas

# The Canterbury Tales

The Prologe

*Here biginneth the Book of the Tales of Caunterbury*

Whan that Aprill with his shoures sote
The droghte of Marche hath perced to the rote,
And bathed every veyne in swich licour
Of which vertu engendred is the flour;
Whan Zephirus eek with his swete breeth
Inspired hath in every holt and heeth
The tendre croppes, and the yonge sonne
Hath in the Ram his halfe cours y-ronne,
And smale fowles maken melodye,
That slepen al the night with open yë
(So priketh hem Nature in hir corages):
Than longen folk to goon on pilgrimages
And palmers for to seken straunge strondes,
To ferne halwes, couthe in sondry londes;
And specially, from every shires ende
Of Engelond, to Caunterbury they wende,
The holy blisful martir for to seke
That hem hath holpen, whan that they were seke.

Geoffrey Chaucer

# The Waste Land

*THE BURIAL OF THE DEAD*
April is the cruellest month, breeding
Lilacs out of the dead land, mixing
Memory and desire, stirring
Dull roots with spring rain.
Winter kept us warm, covering
Earth in forgetful snow, feeding
A little life with dried tubers.
Summer surprised us, coming over the Starnbergersee
With a shower of rain; we stopped in the colonnade,
And went on in sunlight, into the Hofgarten,
And drank coffee, and talked for an hour.
Bin gar keine Russin, stamm' aus Litauen, echt deutsch.
And when we were children, staying at the arch-duke's,
My cousin's, he took me out on a sled,
And I was frightened. He said, Marie,
Marie, hold on tight. And down we went.
In the mountains, there you feel free.
I read, much of the night, and go south in the winter.

Thomas Stearns Eliot

# SPRING SONG

It was as if
someone only had to say
*Abracadabra*
to set alight
the chestnut
candelabra.

Bloom and blossom
everywhere, on furze,
on Queen Anne's lace.
A breeze blew
cherry snows
on the common place.

Weeds on walls;
the long grass
of the long acre:
the elderberry bushes
blazing thanks
to their maker.

Loud leaves of
southside trees,
the reticent buds of ash,
the reach of undergrowth
were voices, voices,
woods' panache.

Cub foxes.
Pheasants galvanised
themselves to sing.
The white thorn flowers
were the light infantry
of Spring

marching down the headlands.
A new flock flowed
through a breach,
a makeshift gate.
And this is heaven:
sunrise through a copper beech.

Peter Fallon

# FLEXIBLE TERRITORIALITY

A recent acclaimed text summarizes the data on territoriality in this way: "Ornithologists thought that the territorial behavior of birds was genetically programmed and static. In fact, territorial behavior is flexible and dynamic." Birds that have been carefully observed (storks, blackbirds, golden-winged sunbirds, pomarine jaegers) vary their territorial behavior flexibly and intelligently: The size of the area defended and monopolized by each bird increases as the food supply decreases; newcomers are driven off when food is scarce but not when it is abundant; the actions of the territory-holder vary appropriately depending on the intentions of the intruder; and the supposedly rigid territorial instincts totally disappear when food is either very abundant or extremely scarce. In brief, birds intelligently or flexibly maintain sufficient territory to meet their needs.

Theodore Xenophon Barber, Ph.D

# Prothalamion

With that, I saw two swans of goodly hue
Come softly swimming down along the Lee;
Two fairer birds I yet did never see.
The snow, which doth the top of Pindus strew,
Did never whiter shew,
Nor Jove himself, when he a swan would be
For love of Leda, whiter did appear:
Yet Leda was they say as white as he,
Yet not so white as these, nor nothing near.
So purely white they were,
That even the gentle stream, the which them bare,
Seemed foul to them, and bade his billows spare
To wet their silken feathers, lest they might
Soil their fair plumes with water not so fair,
And mar their beauties bright,
That shone as heaven's light,
Against their bridal day, which was not long:
Sweet Thames, run softly, till I end my song.

Edmund Spenser

# AN EASTER LILY

Tonight the
sky received
A paschal moon
It came on time
And through half-open
shutters
Its ceremonial radiance
Enters our houses

I for my part
received
An Easter lily
Whose whiteness
Is past belief

Its blossoms
The shape of trumpets
Are mute as swans

But deep and strong as sweat
Is their feral perfume.

Anne
Porter

# I DON'T KNOW OF . . .

I don't know of anything in the entire world more wonderful to look at than a nest with eggs in it. An egg, because it contains life, is the most perfect thing there is. It is beautiful and mysterious. An egg is a far finer thing than a tennis ball or a cake of soap. A tennis ball will always be just a tennis ball. A cake of soap will always be just a cake of soap – until it gets so small nobody wants it and they throw it away. But an egg will someday be a living creature. A swan's egg will open and out will come a little swan. A nest is almost as wonderful and mysterious as an egg. How does a bird know how to make a nest? Nobody ever taught her. How does a bird know how to build a nest?

E. B. White

FEMALE SWAN TURNING HER EGGS EVERY SIX TO EIGHT HOURS

Cob is protecting the pen and her nest

Egg tooth at 0430 AM

THE FIRST CYGNET EMERGES AT 1000 HR

THE SECOND CYGNET

Four cygnets with one egg waiting

THE PEN AND HER CLUTCH

Bonding

Spring sun

Exploring

MOTHER'S WARMTH

Initiation to the pond

THE PEN, FOUR CYGNETS AND ALGAE

# NO SWAN SO FINE

"No water so still as the
dead fountains of Versailles."  No swan,
with swart blind look askance
and gondoliering legs, so fine
as the chintz china one with fawn-
brown eyes and toothed gold
collar on to show whose bird it was.

Lodged in the Louis Fifteenth
candelabrum-tree of cockscomb-
tinted buttons, dahlias,
sea urchins, and everlastings,
it perches on the branching foam
of polished sculptured
flowers – at ease and tall.  The king
is dead.

Marianne Moore

# WHEN THE LIGHT FALLS

When the light falls, it falls on her
In whose rose-gilded chamber
A music strained through mind
Turns everything to measure.

The light that seeks her out
Finds answering light within,
And the two join hands and dance
On either side of her skin.

The lily and the swan
Attend her whiter pride,
While the courtly laurel kneels
To kiss his mantling bride.

Under each cherry-bough
She spreads her silken cloths
At the rumor of a wind,
To gather up her deaths,

For the petals of her heart
Are shaken in a night,
Whose ceremonial art
Is dying into light.

Stanley Kunitz

Pine pollen at dusk

THREE CYGNETS WITH PONDWEEDS

The pen, two cygnets and choke cherry leaves

# THE SWAN

Hawks stir the blood like fiercely ringing bells
or far-off bugles;
even on their perches
they are all latent fury and sheathed power;
and peacocks trail the glory of the world.
But calm, white calm, was born into a swan
to float forever upon moon-smoothed waters
cool placid breast against cool mirrored breast,
and wings curved like great petals
and long throat
bent dreamingly
to listen to the ripple
that widens slowly in a tranquil arrow
reaching the shores, and lisping on the sands.

Elizabeth Coatsworth

# I am the . . .

I am the cygnet to this pale faint swan,
Who chants a doleful hymn to his own death,
And from the organ-pipe of frailty sings
His soul and body to their lasting rest.

William Shakespeare

# THE PERENNIAL RETAINERS

On a pond, a despot swan rules with so tyrannical a rule that no other swan, except the wife of the feared one, dares to enter the water at all. You can catch this terrible tyrant and carry him away before the eyes of all the others, and expect that the remaining birds will breathe an audible sigh of relief and at once proceed to take the bath of which they have been so long deprived. Nothing of the kind occurs. Days pass before the first of these suppressed subjects can pluck up enough courage to indulge in a modest swim hard against the shores of the pond. For a much longer time, nobody ventures into the middle of the water.

Konrad Z. Lorenz

Territory

# THE SONG OF SOLOMON
## CHAPTER 2

I am the rose of Shar'-on, and the lily of the valleys.

2 As the lily among thorns, so is my love among the daughters.

3 As the apple tree among the trees of the wood, so is my beloved among the sons. I sat down under his [1]shadow with great delight, and [a]his fruit was sweet to my taste.

4 He brought me to the [1]banqueting house, and his banner over me was love.

5 [1]Stay me with flagons. [1]comfort me with apples: for I am [3]sick of love.

6 [a]His left hand is under my head, and his right hand doth embrace me.

7 [a]I[1] charge you, O ye daughters of Jerusalem, by the [2]roes, and by the [3]hinds of the field, that ye stir not up, nor awake my love, till he please.

8 The voice of my beloved! behold, he cometh leaping upon the mountains, skipping upon the hills.

9 [a]My beloved is like a [1]roe or a young [2]hart: behold, he standeth behind our wall, he looketh forth at the windows, [3]shewing himself through the lattice.

10 My beloved spake, and said unto me, Rise up, my love, my fair one, and come away.

11 For, lo, the winter is past, the rain is over and gone;

12 The flowers appear on the earth; the time of the singing of birds is come, and the voice of the [1]turtle is heard in our land;

13 The fig tree putteth forth her green figs, and the vines with the tender grape give a good smell. Arise, my love, my fair one, and come away.

The Holy Bible
King James Version

WINTER IS PAST

# SWANS MATING

Even now I wish that you had been there
Sitting beside me on the riverbank:
The cob and his pen sailing in rhythm
Until their small heads met and the final
Heraldic moment dissolved in ripples.

This was a marriage and a baptism,
A holding of breath, nearly a drowning,
Wings spread wide for balance where he trod,
Her feathers full of water and her neck
Under the water like a bar of light.

Michael Longley

# BLACK SWAN

I've feared the rope-thick length of neck,
the hint of wingspan, a shiver
shuffle-dealt like threat, even the orange
webbed feet, the kick
that glides him across the lake, away,
swims deep in myth, deep in what lies
in childhood to define, to overpower.

I cannot answer what difference
this color makes, this dark lack
of silence, the insistence of
his extended neck, his head bowing
to trumpet, almost a nod, almost
gentlemanly as I walk past
towards the mailbox.  Each day,
familiar, there is this shadow, the grace
of his red bill open in acknowledgement.

Lyrae Van Clief-Stefanon

BLACK AUSTRALIAN SWAN WITH SPRING NEST

Turning the eggs

GREEN AND BLACK

# UNDER CYGNUS

Who says I shall not straighten till I bend,
And must be broken if I hope to mend?
Did Samson gain by being chained and blind?
Dark heaven hints at something of the kind,
Seeing that as we beat toward Hercules
Our flank is compassed by the galaxy's,
And we drawn off from our intended course
By a grand reel of stars whose banded force,
Catching us up, makes light of all our loss,
And dances us into the Northern Cross.

Well, if I must surrender and be gay
In the wrong pasture of the Milky Way,
If in the Cross I must resign my Sword,
To hang among the trophies of the Lord,
Let my distinction not consist alone
In having let myself be overthrown.
It was my loves and labors, carried high,
Which drove the flight that heaven turns awry,
My dreams which told the stars what they should tell.
Let the Swan, dying, sing of that as well.

Richard Wilbur

Spring clutch

The family: cob, pen and septulets.

SIX CYGNETS WITH PONDWEEDS

FIVE CYGNETS

Pen and two cygnets

# LEVIATHAN

In that day the Lord with his
[1]sore and great and strong
sword shall punish [2]le-vi'-a-than
the [3]piercing serpent, [a]even le-vi'-
a-than that  [4]crooked serpent; and
he shall slay the [5]dragon that is
in the sea.   Isaiah 27:1

There go the ships: *there is*
that [a]leviathan, [1]*whom thou hast*
[2]made to play therein.
Psalm 104:26

Canst thou draw out [a]levia-
than[1] with an hook?   or his
tongue with a cord *which* thou let-
test down?
2  Canst thou [a]put an [1]hook into
his nose?  or bore his jaw through
with a [2]thorn?   Job 41:1-2

The Holy Bible
King James Version

Snapping turtle (Chelydra serpentina)

# SUMMER

# Fern Hill

Now as I was young and easy under the apple boughs
About the lilting house and happy as the grass was green,
    The night above the dingle starry,
       Time let me hail and climb
    Golden in the heydays of his eyes,
And honoured among wagons I was prince of the apple towns
And once below a time I lordly had the trees and leaves
       Trail with daisies and barley
    Down the rivers of the windfall light.

And as I was green and carefree, famous among the barns
About the happy yard and singing as the farm was home,
    In the sun that is young once only,
       Time let me play and be
    Golden in the mercy of his means,
And green and golden I was huntsman and herdsman, the calves
Sang to my horn, the foxes on the hills barked clear and cold,
    And the sabbath rang slowly
    In the pebbles of the holy streams.

All the sun long it was running, it was lovely, the hay
Fields high as the house, the tunes from the chimneys, it
       was air
    And playing, lovely and watery
       And fire green as grass.
    And nightly under the simple stars
As I rode to sleep the owls were bearing the farm away,
All the moon long I heard, blessed among stables, the night-jars
    Flying with the ricks, and the horses
    Flashing into the dark.

And then to awake, and the farm, like a wanderer white
With the dew, come back, the cock on his shoulder: it was all
    Shining, it was Adam and maiden,
       The sky gathered again
    And the sun grew round that very day.
So it must have been after the birth of the simple light
In the first, spinning place, the spellbound horses walking warm
    Out of the whinnying green stable
    On to the fields of praise.

And honoured among foxes and pheasants by the gay house
Under the new made clouds and happy as the heart was long,
    In the sun born over and over,
       I ran my heedless ways,
    My wishes raced through the house high hay
And nothing I cared, at my sky blue trades, that time allows
In all his tuneful turning so few and such morning songs
    Before the children green and golden
    Follow him out of grace,

Nothing I cared, in the lamb white days, that time would take me
Up to the swallow thronged loft by the shadow of my hand,
    In the moon that is always rising,
       Nor that riding to sleep
    I should hear him fly with the high fields
And wake to the farm forever fled from the childless land.
Oh as I was young and easy in the mercy of his means,
    Time held me green and dying
    Though I sang in my chains like the sea.

Dylan Thomas

# PASTORAL

I go copying mountains and rivers and clouds:
I shake out my fountain pen, remark
on a bird flying upward
or a spider alive in his workshop of floss,
with no thought in my head; I am air,
I am limitless air where the wheat tosses,
and am moved by an impulse to fly, the uncertain
direction of leaves, the round
eye of the motionless fish in the cove,
statues that soar through the clouds,
the rain's multiplications.

I see only a summer's
transparency, I sing nothing but wind,
while history creaks on its carnival floats
hoarding medals and shrouds
and passes me by, and I stand by myself
in the spring, knowing nothing but rivers.

Shepherd-boy, shepherd-boy, don't you know
that they wait for you?

I know and I know it: but here by the water
in the crackle and flare of cicadas,
I must wait for myself, as they wait for me there:
I also would see myself coming
and know in the end how it feels to me
when I come to the place where I wait for my coming
and turn back to my sleep and die laughing.

Pablo Neruda
Translated by Alastair Reid

# "Hope" is the Thing with Feathers

"Hope" is the thing with feathers -
That perches in the soul -
And sings the tune without the words -
And never stops - at all -

And sweetest - in the Gale - is heard-
And sore must be the storm -
That could abash the little Bird
That kept so many warm -

I've heard it in the chillest land -
And on the strangest Sea -
Yet, never, in Extremity,
It asked a crumb - of Me.

Emily Dickinson

# DRAGONFLY

To which the voice did urge reply:
"To-day I saw the dragon-fly
Come from the wells where he did lie.

"An inner impulse rent the veil
Of his old husk; from head to tail
Came out clear plates of sapphire mail.

"He dried his wings; like gauze they grew;
Thro' crofts and pastures wet with dew
A living flash of light he flew."

Alfred Lord Tennyson

# TO A BUTTERFLY

Already in midsummer
I miss your feet and fur.
Poor simple creature that you were,
What have you become!

Your slender person curled
About an apple twig
Rebounding to the winds' clear jig
Gave up the world

In favor of obscene
Gray matter, rode that ark
Until (as at the chance remark
Of Father Sheen)

Shining awake to slough
Your old life.  And soon four
Dapper stained glass windows bore
You up – *Enough*.

Goodness, how tired one grows
Just looking through a prism:
Allegory, symbolism.
I've tried, Lord knows,

To keep from seeing double,
Blushed for whenever I did,
Prayed like a boy my cheek he hid
By manly stubble.

I caught you in a net
And first pierced your disguise
How many years ago?  Time flies,
I am not yet

Proof against rigmarole.
Those frail wings, those antennae!
The day you hover without any
Tincture of soul,

Red monarch, swallowtail,
Will be the day my own
Wiles gather dust.  Each will have flown
The other's jail.

James Merrill

# The Black Swan

Black on flat water past the jonquil lawns
        Riding, the black swan draws
A private chaos warbling in its wake,
Assuming, like a fourth dimension, splendor
That calls the child with white ideas of swans
        Nearer to that green lake
    Where every paradox means wonder.

Though the black swan's arched neck is like
        A question-mark on the lake,
The swan outlaws all possible questioning:
A thing in itself, like love, like submarine
Disaster, or the first sound when we wake;
        And the swan-song it sings
    Is the huge silence of the swan.

Illusion: the black swan knows how to break
        Through expectation, beak
Aimed now at its own breast, now at its image,
And move across over lives, if the lake is life,
And by the gentlest turning of its neck
Transform, in time, time's damage;
To less than a black plume, time's grief.

Enchanter: the black swan has learned to enter
        Sorrow's lost secret center
Where like a maypole separate tragedies
Are wound about a tower of ribbons, and where
The central hollowness is that pure winter
        That does not change but is
    Always brilliant ice and air.

Always the black swan moves on the lake; always
        The blond child seems to gaze
As the tall emblem pivots and rides out
To the opposite side, always.  The child upon
The bank, hands full of difficult marvels, stays
        Forever to cry aloud
    In anguish: I love the black swan.

James Merrill

THREE MONTHS

THE YEARLINGS

WHITE-CHEEKED PINTAILS

Pursuit of geese

# DUSK

*Crépuscule*

*To Mademoiselle Marie Laurencin*

Brushed by the shadows of the dead
On grass where failing daylight falls
The lady harlequin's stripped bare
Admiring herself in a still pool

A twilight juggler a charlatan
Boasts tricks that he knows how to play
Pale as milk the studding stars
Stand in the tall uncolored air

Harlequin pallid on his small stage
Greets the audience first of all
Bohemian sorcerers a train
Of fairies and prestidigitals

Reaching up to unhook a star
He whirls it round with outstretched arm
While cymbals mark a measured beat
Hanging from a hanged man's feet

The sightless one croons to a child
The hind and her troop of fawns pass by
The dwarf sulks at the growing thrust
Of Harlequin the Trismegist

Guillaume Apollinaire

# SUMMERTIME

Summertime (From "Porgy And Bess")

Summertime, an' the livin' is easy,
Fish are jumpin', an' the cotton is high.
Oh yo' daddy's rich, an' yo' ma is good lookin',
So hush, little baby, don' yo' cry.

One of these mornin's You goin' to rise up singin',
Then you'll spread yo' wings-an' you'll take the sky.
But till that mornin' there's a nothin' can harm you-
With Daddy an' Mammy stand-in' by.

Dubose and Dorothy Heyward
George and Ira Gershwin

# MEMORIA

I have never heard them;
I shall never hear –
Still and echo falling
When the night is clear;
In the darkness wakes me
Like a trumpet's call:
Wild swans crying
Southward in the fall.

Louise McNeill

# THE SWAN

Out on the bay, a swan
glides like a hunk of ice,
neck curved like the bride's
wrist cutting her wedding cake;
its wings and fluffy back are clouds
upon the waves, reflected from above.
Beneath the surface,
webbed, grey feet churn hard
in cold, muddy water.

Hannu Niklander

# THE SWAN

Scholars call the masculine swan a cob;
I call him a narcissistic snob.
He looks in the mirror over and over,
And claims to have never heard of Pavlova.

Ogden Nash

# THE SWAN

Swan, I'd like you to tell me your whole story!
Where you first appeared, and what dark sand you are going
toward,
and where you sleep at night, and what you are looking
for....
It's morning, swan, wake up, climb in the air, follow me!
I know of a country that spiritual flatness does not control,
nor constant depression,
and those alive are not afraid to die.
There wildflowers come up through the leafy floor,
and the fragrance of "I am he" floats on the wind.
There the bee of the heart stays deep inside the flower,
and cares for no other thing.

Kabir
Translated by Robert Bly

# THE SWAN

This toiling labor for a goal not yet achieved
that like a heavy burden hinders every step,
is like the swan's ungainly gait

which illuminates this dying, this no longer
holding on to the ground on which we daily stand,
so like his anxious lowering of himself —:

into the waters that receive him gently,
and then, happy and bygone, begin to lift him
wave to wave, receding soundlessly beneath him,
while he, infinitely still and self-assured
and ever more mature, with regal bearing,
deigns to be borne serenely drifting by.

Rainer Marie Rilke

# LEDA

Come not with kisses
not with caresses
of hands and lips and murmurings;
come with a hiss of wings
and sea-touch tip of a beak
and treading of wet, webbed, wave-working feet
into the marsh-soft belly.

D. H. Lawrence

# SUMMER SOLSTICE

I watch the shuffle of leaves
sorting out sky from the slow crawl
of sunlight up the bark of two tall elms.
How long is this day?
How impossible the project of the pines
to square the circle of light
I sit in, with the steady lift
and lower of their boughs.
As if the bracken had been given voice,
a crow calls out and rises.
If this were the end, would I sit up
with an immense alertness
and ask for three more days?
Among so many trees, I imagine
I am a tree myself, a sycamore
struck by lightning, charred bark
curling to the duff.
Raw to weather and desire,
I am pared down to nerve and fever.
I watch the light and wait
for the year to turn me over.

Maggie Anderson

Moulting

# THE SWAN

## I

Andromache, I think of you!  This poor
Rivulet where your fabled sorrows gleam,
This downscale Simois where as of yore
Your widow's tears forever swell the stream

Has watered my green memory as well,
Suddenly, at the Place du Carrousel.
Mercurial as human feelings are,
The shapes of cities alter faster far:

Old Paris is no more.  I only see
Huts full of bric-a-brac in my mind's eye,
Barrels heaped up, and columns whose rough stone
Splashes of muddy water have turned green.

Caged animals were on display just there;
And there I saw once in the clear cold dawn
When early workers raise a hurricane
Of blackish dust in the still silent air,

A swan.  Out of its cage, it dragged its feet
Along the bone-dry sidewalk; glossy white
Pinions trailed the pebbles in its wake.
Near a dry brook-bed opening its beak,

Skittishly flirting feathers in a bath
Of dust, and heartsick for its native lake,
"Oh, water, rain on me!  Oh thunder, break!"
The wretched swan was saying. Fatal myth

Emblazoned like an emblem in the sky –
The tremulous writhing neck, the avid head
Outstretched to tell its troubles straight to God –
Cruel and ironic, still in the mind's eye!

## II

Paris changes, not my old distress.
New buildings in construction, scaffoldings,
My memories with their stony heaviness,
Old districts – all are now symbolic things.

Thus before the Louvre even now
The image rises: my great swan, its motions
Dignified, mad as any displaced person's,
Obsessed with endless longing – then of you,

Andromache!  No longer shelter in
Your lost lord's arms, slave of Achilles' son,
You huddle in an ecstasy of grief
To mourn for Hector – Helenus's wife!

I think of a consumptive Negress, gaunt
And haggard, scouring the filthy street
For the lost palm trees of her native haunt,
For Africa behind a wall of sleet.

Of losses that can never be made good,
Never! of people draining a whole gulf
Of grief, yes, suckling Sorrow like a wolf;
Of skinny orphans who like flowers fade!

So in the forest of my mind's exile
An ancient memory blows its horn.  The sound
Conjures up sailors shipwrecked on an isle,
And prisoners, victims, others without end!

Charles Baudelaire
Translated by Rachel Hadas

# THE DESIRED SWAN-SONG

Swans sing before they die – 'twere no bad thing
Should certain persons die before they sing.

Samuel Taylor Coleridge

# SWAN

FAR-OFF
at the core of space
at the quick of time
beats
and goes still
the great swan upon the waters of all endings
the swan within vast chaos, within the electron.

For us
no longer he swims calmly
nor clacks across the forces furrowing a great gay
trail
of happy energy,
nor is he nesting passive upon the atoms,
nor flying north desolative icewards
to the sleep of ice,
nor feeding in the marshes,
nor honking horn-like into the twilight. –

But he stoops, now
in the dark
upon us;
he is treading our women
and we men are put out
as the vast white bird
furrows our featherless women
with unknown shocks
and stamps his black marsh-feet on their white
and marshy flesh.

D. H. Lawrence

# BLUE

The blue door that the skylark opens –
a creaking of heavenly hinges.
The infinite recession of sky
painted blue by its own emptiness.
Metaphors for the ungraspable
essence of azure. 'Watch your pen,' is
what I say to myself.  'That colour
will run away with it, a mirage
of water in the yellow desert.
You will write of blue where there is none.'
Passing over the ocean, the
boat throws white spray from its bow.   The wake
curves green behind.  Looking down, you see
the brown of weed, the silver of fish
scattering from their pasture.  The ink
flowing is blue-black, not blue as you think.

Edward Lucie-Smith

# FALL

# NOW THE LEAVES ARE FALLING FAST

Now the leaves are falling fast,
Nurse's flowers will not last;
Nurses to the graves are gone,
And the prams go rolling on.

Whispering neighbours, left and right,
Pluck us from the real delight;
And the active hands must freeze
Lonely on the separate knees.

Dead in hundreds at the back
Follow wooden in our track,
Arms raised stiffly to reprove
In false attitudes of love.

Starving through the leafless wood
Trolls run scolding for their food;
And the nightingale is dumb,
And the angel will not come.

Cold, impossible, ahead
Lifts the mountain's lovely head
Whose white waterfall could bless
Travellers in their last distress.

Wystan Hugh Auden

# AUTUMN LEAVES

The autumn trees stretch out their arms,
Filled with brilliant jewels,
Ruby and gold, some emerald,
Fashioned from fairy tools.

Intricately cut by unseen hand
Filigreed with care,
An offering to the cold north wind,
Greedy for the rare.

The jewels blaze high on the hill,
And smoulder on the plain.
The north wind rushes from the sky,
Unable to refrain,

From clutching every brilliant gem
Close in his lead-gray hand.
He ties them to long threads of mist,
And whirls them over land.

But one by one they drop away
And flutter back to earth,
Where they will crumble into dust,
A gift for spring's rebirth.

Margaret Phillips Succop

# Spring And Fall:
# To a Young Child

Márgarét, are you griéving
Over Goldengrove unleaving?
Leáves, líke the things of man, you
With your fresh thoughts care for, can you?
Áh! As the heart grows older
It will come to such sights colder
By and by, nor spare a sigh
Though worlds of wanwood leafmeal lie;
And yet you wíll weep and know why.
Now no matter, child, the name:
Sórrow's spríngs áre the same.
Nor mouth had, no nor mind, expressed
What heart heard of, ghost guessed:
It ís the blight man was born for,
It is Margaret you mourn for.

Gerard Manley Hopkins

# THISTLEDOWN

First clan of autumn, thistleball on a stem
Between forefinger and thumb,
Known for the seeds
That make a wish come true when the light last of them
Into air blown subsides,

Feathery sphere of seeds, frail brain
On prickly spine,
I feared their dissipation, deeds of this crown aspin,
Words from a high-flown talker, pale brown
Thistledown.

Yet when, bewildered what to want
Past the extravagant
Notion of wanting, I puffed
And the soft cluster broke and spinning went
More channels than I knew, aloft

In the wide air to lift its lineage
Ha! how the Scotch flower's spendthrift
Stars drifted down
Many to tarn or turf, but ever a canny one
On the stem left

To remind me of what I had wished:
That none should have clung, lest summer, thistle-bewitched,
Dry up, be done
– And the whole of desire not yet into watched
Air at a breath blown!

James Merrill

# HOAR FROST

The last cold lilies cringed
Before this challenge hinted;
Our raptures have repented,
Death has been avenged.
Now beauty; stern as time
Usurps her rival beauty,
Effulgent, wild.  No pity
Is scattered with her rime
Upon the earth's frail tide,
Inexorably sealing
Autumn's distilling
Of the summer's bright pride.
Bend before this chaste
Power, stark and subtle,
Now passion is effaced
And pride is futile.

Morton Dauwen Zabel

# AUTUMN EVENING

In the late day shining cobwebs trailed from my fingers
I could not see the far ends somewhere to the south
gold light hung for a long time in the wild clematis
called old man's beard along the warm wall
now smoke from my fire drifts across the red sun setting
half the bronze leaves still hold to the walnut trees
marjoram joy of the mountains flowers again
even in the light frosts of these nights
and there are mushrooms though the moon is new
and though shadows whiten on the grass before morning
and cowbells sound in the dusk from winter pastures

W. S. Merwin

# HALF OF LIFE

With its yellow pears
And wild roses everywhere
The shore hangs in the lake,
O gracious swans,
And drunk with kisses
You dip your heads
In the sobering holy water.

Ah, where will I find
Flowers, come winter,
And where the sunshine
And shade of the earth?
Walls stand cold
And speechless, in the wind
The weathervanes creak.

Friedrich Hölderlin
    Translated and Introduced by
        Richard Sieburth

# IMMORTAL AUTUMN

I speak this poem now with grave and level voice
In praise of autumn of the far-horn-winding fall
I praise the flower-barren fields the clouds the tall
Unanswering branches where the wind makes sullen noise

I praise the fall it is the human season now
No more the foreign sun does meddle at our earth
Enforce the green and thaw the frozen soil to birth
Nor winter yet weigh all with silence the pine bough

But now in autumn with the black and outcast crows
Share we the spacious world the whispering year is gone
There is more room to live now the once secret dawn
Comes late by daylight and the dark unguarded goes

Between the mutinous brave burning of the leaves
And winter's covering of our hearts with his deep snow
We are alone there are no evening birds we know
The naked moon the tame stars circle at out eaves

It is the human season on this sterile air
Do words outcarry breath the sound goes on and on
I hear a dead Man's cry from autumn long since gone

I cry to you beyond this bitter air.

Archibald MacLeish

# THE WILD SWANS AT NORFOLK

To begin with there are
No wild swans at Norfolk,
This other Norfolk
Where James Laughlin lives
With his red-haired Ann.

There are towhees and wrens
And soft yellow sapsuckers
And Blackburnian warblers
And gray owls and barred owls
And flickers but there are
No wild swans
I can invent the swans.

They wheel on thunder's
Hundred throbbing wings
Down the sweet curve
Of Tobey Pond, pounding
The blocks of air
As trains in my childhood
Pounded their rails.

They are real wild swans;
And even though this summer
I turn forty and am deserted
By the young woman I love,
I have grown sick of emblems.

I have seen this place
On the map, and the names of
The people of Norfolk appear
On voting lists and tax rolls.

Hear how the swans converse
(As they break wing for landing)
In a rude, lightning tongue.
I cannot understand,
But clearly the swans know
What they are talking about.

Hayden Carruth

# THE DYING SWAN

The plain was grassy, wild and bare,
Wide, wild, and open to the air,
Which had built up everywhere
An under-roof of doleful gray.
With an inner voice the river ran,
Adown it floated a dying swan,
And loudly did it lament.
It was the middle of the day.
Even the weary wind went on,
And took the reed-tops as it went.

Some blue peaks in the distance rose,
And white against the cold-white sky,
Shone out their crowning snows.
One willow over the river wept,
And shook the wave as the wind did sigh;
Above in the wind was the swallow,
Chasing itself at its own wild will,
And far thro' the marish green and still
The tangled water-courses slept,
Shot over with purple, and green, and yellow.

The wild swan's death-hymn took the soul
Of that waste place with joy
Hidden in sorrow: at first to the ear
The warble was low, and full and clear;
And floating about the under-sky.
Prevailing in weakness, the coronach stole
Sometimes afar, and sometimes anear;
But anon her awful jubilant voice,
With a music strange and manifold,
Flow'd forth on a carol free and bold;
As when a mighty people rejoice
With shawms, and with cymbals, and harps of
Gold,
And the tumult of their acclaim is roll'd
Thro' the open gates of the city afar,
To the Shepard who watcheth the evening star.
And the creeping mosses and clambering weeds,
And the willow-branches hoar and dank,
And the wavy swell of the soughing reeds,
And the wave-worn horns of the echoing bank,
And the silvery marish-flowers that throng
The desolate creeks and pools among,
Were flooded over with eddying song.

Alfred Lord Tennyson

# ANGUS OG

Angus Og ["Angus the Young"] is the Gaelic god of love. And as love always makes people youthful, the name fits. Four bright birds hover about his head—the embodiment of his kisses. Anyone hearing the songs of these birds falls hopelessly in love. Angus is the son of the Dagda ("the Good God"), the Supreme Being. Angus himself is constantly in love.

Once Angus fell dangerously ill from "love sickness" for a young girl, and his mother, Boanna, searched all of Ireland to find her without success. Then the great Dagda was called in, but even he could not find her. The Dagda asked Bov the Red for assistance, as Bov knew all mysteries. Bov himself did not know where she was, but he eventually found her at the Lake of the Dragon's Mouth.

Angus then went to see Bov and they feasted together for three days. Eager to see his beloved, Angus begged Bov to take him to her. When they arrived at the Lake of the Dragon's Mouth, Angus saw a hundred and fifty beautiful maidens, the most beautiful in the world, walking in pairs, each pair linked by a chain of pure gold. One maiden was taller than the rest; this was the girl that Angus loved. Angus was seized with desire and wanted to carry her off. However, Bov warned that she would not be separated from the others without difficulty. The girl's name was Caer, and she was the daughter of an unrelated semidivine prince of the province of Connacht.

Angus went to see the king and queen of Connacht to seek their assistance in winning the hand of Caer, but even the king and queen had no power to help. What irony! Angus, who made all lovers fall in love, was unable to win the hand of his own beloved without help. The king and queen, however, did agree to send a message to Caer's father asking for Caer's hand on Angus's behalf.

Angus approached Caer's father to ask her hand, but the older man refused to see the young suitor. The armies of the Dagda and the king of Connacht besieged the home of Caer's father and took him prisoner. However, Caer's father finally explained that he had no power to give his daughter in marriage; her magic was more powerful than his. He further explained that Caer lived six months out of every year in the form of a woman and the other six months in the form of a swan. On the feast of Samhain, Caer would be found again at the lake with the other girls, all in the form of swans.

Angus went to the lake on the feast of Samhain and begged Caer, now a swan, to be his bride. She asked who he was and he explained that he was Angus Og, the god of love. As he spoke his name, he himself was transformed into a swan, and he and Caer lived together forever after. Angus now often appears to lovers in the guise of the swan, and this is why lovers like to meet near lakes.

J. F. Bierlein

# THE SILVER SWANNE

The silver swan, who living had no note.
When death approach'd, unlock'd her silent throat;
Leaning her breast against the reedy shore,
Thus sang her first and last, and sung no more.
Farewell, all joys; O Death, come close mine eyes;
More geese than swans now live, more fools than wise.

Orlando Gibbons

# THE SWAN AND GOOSE

A rich man bought a Swan and Goose –
That for song and this for use.
It chanced his simple-minded cook
One night the Swan for Goose mistook.
But in the dark about to chop
The Swan in two above the crop,
He heard the lyric note, and stayed
The action of the fatal blade.

And thus we see a proper tune
Is sometimes very opportune.

Aesop
Translated by William Ellery Leonard

# THE WILD SWANS AT COOLE

The trees are in their autumn beauty,
The woodland paths are dry,
Under the October twilight the water
Mirrors a still sky;
Upon the brimming water among the stones
Are nine-and-fifty swans.

The nineteenth autumn has come upon me
Since I first made my count;
I saw, before I had well finished,
All suddenly mount
And scatter wheeling in great broken rings
Upon their clamorous wings.

I have looked upon those brilliant creatures,
And now my heart is sore.
All's changed since I, hearing at twilight,

The first time on this shore,
The bell-beat of their wings above my head,
Trod with a lighter tread.

Unwearied still, lover by lover,
They paddle in the cold
Companionable streams or climb the air;
Their hearts have not grown old;
Passion or conquest, wander where they will,
Attend upon them still.

But now they drift on the still water
Mysterious, beautiful;
Among what rushes will they build,
By what lake's edge or pool
Delight men's eyes when I awake some day
To find they have flown away?

William Butler Yeats

# THE SONG OF FIONMALA

The old fables of Valkyries were misunderstood when Christianity had cast these damsels from heaven, and the stories were modified to account for the transformation. The sweet maidens no more swam of their own free will in the crystal waves, but swam thus through the force of an enchantment they were unable to break. Thus, in the Irish legend of Fionmala, the daughter of King Lir, on the death of the mother of Fingula (Fionmala) and her brothers, their father married the wicked Aoife, who, through spite, transforms the children of Lir into swans, which must float on the waters for centuries, till the first mass-bell tingles. Who does not remember Tom Moore's verses on the legend? —

Silent, O Moyle, be the roar of thy water;
Break not, ye breezes, your chain of repose,
While, murmuring mournfully, Lir's lovely daughter
Tells to the night-star the tale of her woes.
When shall the swan, her death-note singing,
Sleep with wings in darkness furl'd?
When will heaven, its sweet bells ringing,
Call my spirit from this stormy world?

Sadly, O Moyle, to thy winter-wave weeping,
Fate bids me languish long ages away;
Yet still in her darkness doth Erin lie sleeping,
Still doth the pure light its dawning delay.
When will that day-star, mildly springing,
Warm our isle with peace and love?
When will heaven, its sweet bells ringing,
Call my spirit to the fields above?

Sabine Baring-Gould

# THE EXTERNAL SOUL IN FOLK-TALES

Another Tartar poem describes how the hero Kartaga grappled with the Swan-woman. Long they wrestled. Moons waxed and waned and still they wrestled; years came and went, and still the struggle went on. But the piebald horse and the black horse knew that the Swan-woman's soul was not in her. Under the black earth flow nine seas; where the seas meet and form one, the sea comes to the surface of the earth. At the mouth of the nine seas rises a rock of copper; it rises to the surface of the ground, it rises up between heaven and earth, this rock of copper. At the foot of the copper rock is a black chest, in the black chest is a golden casket, and in the golden casket is the soul of the Swan-woman. Seven little birds are the soul of the Swan-woman; if the birds are killed the Swan-woman will die straightway. So the horses ran to the foot of the copper rock, opened the black chest, and brought back the golden casket. Then the piebald horse turned himself into a bald-headed man, opened the golden casket, and cut off the heads of the seven birds. So the Swan-woman died.

Sir James George Frazer

# ODETTE

"As if to echo in their motion the roundness of the moon that bathed them in silver light, the swans were dancing in a ring. Their dance was the perfect union of delirium and control, of purity and abandon, of nature and civilization. How did they put together so gentle a thing with so much power, so powerful a thing with so much grace? It was almost an eastern rite, and yet, they were swans, and yet....

"Then he could not believe his eyes, and though he insisted to himself that he was dreaming, the dream was so beautiful that he believed it more than what was real. The swans had become women, and the women had then become swans, until he could not separate them or distinguish between their forms.

Mark Helprin

# THE SWAN-MAIDEN

The classic swan myths must be considered in greater detail.  They are numerous, for each Greek tribe had its own favourite myths, and additional fables were being constantly imported into religion from foreign sources.  The swan was with the Greeks the bird of the Muses, and therefore also of Apollo.  When the golden-haired deity was born, swans came from the golden stream of Pactolus, and seven times wheeled about Delos, uttering songs of joy.

Seven times, on snowy pinions, circle round
The Delian shores, and skim along the ground:
The vocal birds, the favourites of the Nine,
In strains melodious hail the birth divine.
Oft as they carol on resounding wings,
To soothe Latona's pangs, as many strings
Apollo fitted to the warbling lyre
In aftertimes; but ere the sacred choir
Of circling swans another concert sung,
In melting notes, the power immortal sprung
To glorious birth.

Sabine Baring-Gould

# WAYLAND AND THE VALKYRS

The Valkyrs were supposed to take frequent flights to earth in swan plumage, which they would throw off when they came to a secluded stream, that they might indulge in a bath. Any mortal surprising them thus, and securing their plumage, could prevent them from leaving the earth, and could even force these proud maidens to mate with him if such were his pleasure.

It is related that three of the Valkyrs, Olrun, Alvit, and Svanhvit, were once sporting in the waters, when suddenly the three brothers Egil, Slagfinn, and Völund, or Wayland the smith, came upon them, and securing their swan plumage, the young men forced them to remain upon earth and become their wives. The Valkyrs, thus detained, remained with their husbands nine years, but at the end of that time, recovering their plumage, or the spell being broken in some other way, they effected their escape.

> "There they stayed
> Seven winters through;
> But all the eighth
> Were with longing seized;
> And in the ninth
> Fate parted them.
> The maidens yearned
> For the murky wood,
> The young Alvit,
> Fate to fulfil."

Lay of Völund (Thorpe's tr.)

The brothers felt the loss of their wives extremely, and two of them, Egil and Slagfinn, putting on their snow shoes, went in search of their loved ones, disappearing in the cold and foggy regions of the North. The third brother, Völund, however, remained at home, knowing all search would be of no avail, and he found solace in the contemplation of a ring which Alvit had given him as a love-token, and he indulged the constant hope that she would return.

H. A. Guerber

# PARZIVAL

Many envoys from distant lands made their way to her, but she abjured all men other than the one assigned to her by God -
that man's love she was pleased to cherish.

This lady was Princess in Brabant. A husband was sent from Munsalvaesche. Destined for her by God, he was brought by the Swan and taken ashore at Antwerp. He proved to be all she could wish for. He was a man of breeding and was inevitably accounted outstanding for looks and courage in all the kingdoms to which knowledge of him came. A courtly, perspicacious, tactful man. One who gave sincerely and generously without wincing, as a person he was without fault.

The lady of the land received him graciously. Now hear what he had to say. It was heard by rich and poor, who were standing here, there and everywhere.

'My lady Duchess,' he said. 'If I am to be lord of this land, I have left as much behind me. Now hear what I wish to beg of you. *Never ask who I am!* – Then I can stay with you. But if I am chosen for your questioning you will have lost my love. If you cannot take this warning, then may God remind me of He knows what.' She gave a woman's pledge – which thanks to her affection later proved infirm – that if God left her her reason she would do her husband's bidding and never go against what he had asked.

That night he knew her love. He then became Prince in Brabant. The wedding celebrations went magnificently. Many lords received at his hands the fiefs to which they had title. That same man became a good judge. And he often practised chivalry and irresistibly claimed the palm.

Together they got lovely children. There are many people in Brabant today who are well informed about this pair – her receiving him, his departure – they know that her question banished him and how long he had been there. And indeed he was very loth to go. But his friend the Swan brought back a small and handy skiff. Of his precious heirlooms he left a sword, horn and ring. Then Loherangrin [Lohengrin] went away. If we are going to do right by this story he was Parzival's son. He travelled over paths and water back to the keeping of the Gral.

Wolfram Von Eschenbach
Translated by A.T. Hatto

# RUDIGER: BALLADS AND METRICAL TALES

Bright on the mountain's heathy slope
    The day's last splendours shine,
And rich with many a radiant hue
    Gleam gaily on the Rhine.

And many a one from Waldhurst's walls
    Along the river stroll'd,
As ruffling o'er the pleasant stream
The evening gales came cold.

So as they stray'd a swan they saw
    Sail stately up and strong,
And by a silver chain he drew
    A little boat along.

Whose streamer to the gentle breeze
    Long floating flutter'd light;
Beneath whose crimson canopy
    There lay reclined a knight.

With arching crest and swelling breast
    On sail'd the stately swan.
And lightly up the parting tide
    The little boat came on.

And onward to the shore they drew,
    Where having left the knight,
The little boat adown the stream
    Fell soon beyond the sight.

Was never a knight in Waldhurst's walls
    Could with this stranger vie,
    Was never a youth at aught esteem'd
    When Rudiger was by.

Was never a maid in Waldhurst's walls
    might match with Margaret;
    Her cheek was fair, her eyes were dark,
    Her silken locks like jet.

And many a rich and noble youth
    Had sought to win the fair,
    But never a rich and noble youth
    Could rival Rudiger.

At every tilt and tourney he
    Still bore away the prize;
    For knightly feats superior still,
    And knightly courtesies.

His gallant feats, his looks, his love,
    Soon won the willing fair;
    And soon did Margaret become
    The wife of Rudiger. . .

                Robert Southey

# ON THE GARDEN WALL

OH, once I walked a garden
In dreams. 'Twas yellow grass.
And many orange-trees grew there
In sand as white as glass.
The curving, wide wall-border
Was marble, like the snow.
I walked that wall a fairy-prince
And, pacing quaint and slow,
Beside me were my pages,
Two giant, friendly birds.
Half swan they were, half peacock.
They spake in courtier-words.
Their inner wings a chariot,
Their outer wings for flight,
They lifted me from dreamland.
We bade those trees good-night.
Swiftly above the stars we rode.
I looked below me soon.
The white-walled garden I had ruled
Was one lone flower – the moon.

Vachel Lindsay

# FANNY

The dying swan by northern lakes
   Sing's [Sings] its wild death song,
 sweet and clear,
And as the solemn music breaks
O'er hill and glen dissolves in air;
Thus musical thy soft voice came,
Thus trembled on thy tongue my name.

Like sunburst through the ebon cloud,
   Which veils the solemn midnight sky,
Piercing cold evening's sable shroud,
   Thus came the first glance of that eye;
But like the adamantine rock,
My spirit met and braved the shock.

Let memory the boy recall
   Who laid his heart upon they shrine,
When far away his footsteps fall,
   Think that he deem'd thy charms divine;
A victim on love's alter [altar] slain,
By witching eyes which looked disdain.

            Edgar Allan Poe

# POEM

The swans on the river, a great
flotilla in the afternoon sun
in October again.

In a fantasy, Yeats saw himself appear
to Maud Gonne as a swan,
his plumage fanning his desire.

One October at Coole Park
he counted fifty-nine wild swans.
He flushed them unto a legend.

*Lover by lover* is how he said they flew,
but one of them must have been without a mate.
Why did he not observe that?

We talk about Zeus and Leda and Yeats
as if they were real people, we identify constellations
as if they were drawn there on the night.

Cygnus and Castor & Pollux
are only ways of looking at
scatterings of starry matter,

a god putting on swan-flesh
to enter a mortal girl
is only a way of looking at love-trouble.

The violence and calm of these big fowl!
When I am not with you
I am always the fifty-ninth.

William Meredith

# SWANS ON THE RIVER AYR

Under the cobbled bridge the white swans float,
Slow in their perilous pride.  Once long ago,
Led as a child along some Sunday lake,
I met these great birds, dabbling the stagnant shore.
We fed them bread from paper bags.  They came,
Dipping their heads to take the stale slices
Out of our hands.  Look! Said the grownups, but
The child wept and flung the treacherous loaf.
Swans in a dream had no such docile eyes,
No humble beaks to touch a child's fingers.

In Ayr I linger on the cobbled bridge
And watch the birds.  I will not tamper with them,
These ailing spirits clipped to live in cities
Whom we have tamed and made as sad as geese.
All swans are only relics of those birds
Who sail the tideless waters of the mind;
Who traveled once the waters of the earth,
Infecting dreams, helping the child to grow;
And who for ages, seeing witless man
Deck the rocks with gifts to make them mild,
Sensed the disaster to their uncaught lives,
And streamed shoreward like a white armada
With heads reared back to strike and wings like knives.

Mary Oliver

# Swan and Shadow

```
                    Dusk
                  Above the
            water hang the
                     loud
                    flies
                    Here
                  O so
                  gray
                  then
               What              A pale signal will appear
               When          Soon before its shadow fades
              Where          Here in this pool of opened eye
              In us      No Upon us As at the very edges
            of where we take shape in the dark air
             this object bares its image awakening
                 ripples of recognition that will
                   brush darkness up into light
       even after this bird this hour both drift by atop the perfect sad instant now
                       already passing out of sight
                   toward yet-untroubled reflection
               this image bears its object darkening
             into memorial shades Scattered bits of
               light       No of water Or something across
               water          Breaking up No Being regathered
                soon            Yet by then a swan will have
                gone               Yes out of mind into what
                 vast
                   pale
                    hush
                     of a
                    place
                      past
             sudden dark as
                if a swan
                   sang
```

John Hollander

# EPILOGUE

## THE SILVER SWAN

As the full moon rises
The swan sings
In sleep
On the lake of the mind.

Kenneth Rexroth

# BIBLIOGRAPHY

## PROLOGUE

Nathan, Leonard
*Diary of a Left-Handed Birdwatcher*
Copyright © 1996 by Leonard Nathan
Excerpt reprinted from *Diary of a Left-Handed Birdwatcher Pg 15*
Used with the permission of Graywolf Press
Saint Paul, Minnesota.

## WINTER

Rexroth, Kenneth
*The Collected Longer Poems of Kenneth Rexroth*
"Leda Hidden"
Copyright © 1967 by Kenneth Rexroth
Reprinted by permission of New Directions Publishing Corp.
New York, NY
Wilbur, Richard
*Ceremony And Other Poems*
"Year's End"
Copyright © 1949 and Renewed 1977, by Richard Wilbur,
Reprinted by permission of Harcourt, Inc.
Orlando, FL
Emerson, Ralph Waldo
*The Complete Poems of Ralph Waldo Emerson*
"The Snow-Storm"
Houghton Mifflin Company, 1903
Boston, MA
Succop, Margaret Phillips
*Climb To The Stars*
"A Winter Day"
Dorrance & Company, Inc.
Copyright © 1952
Philadelphia, Pa.
Wylie, Elinor
*The Collected Poems of Elinor Wylie*
"Velvet Shoes"
Copyright © 1929
Alfred A. Knopf, Inc.
New York, NY

Clief-Stefanon, Lyrae Van
*Black Swan*
"Leda"
Copyright © 2002
Reprinted by permission of the University of Pittsburgh Press
Pittsburgh, PA
Rilke, Rainer Maria
*New Poems [1908]: The Other Part*
"Leda"
Translated by Edward Snow
North Point Press
Farrar, Straus, and Giroux, LLC
New York, NY
Bogan, Louise
*THE BLUE ESTUARIES*
"Winter Swan"
Copyright © 1968 by Louise Bogan
Copyright renewed by Ruth Limmer
Reprinted by permission of Farrar, Straus and Giroux, LLC
New York, NY
Eliot, T.S.
*The Quartets*
"Little Gidding"
Copyright © 1942 by T.S. Eliot and renewed 1970 by Esme Valerie Eliot
Excerpt from "Little Gidding" Part l, in Four Quartets
Reprinted by permission of Harcourt Inc.
New York, NY
Hollander, John
*Selected Poetry*
"Metathalamia"
Copyright © 1993
Used by permission of Alfred A. Knopf, Inc.,
A division of Random House Inc.
New York, NY
Randall, Jarrell
*The Complete Poems*
"The Black Swan"
Copyright © Renewed 1969, renewed 1997 by Mary Von S. Jarrell
Reprinted by permission of Farrar, Straus and Giroux, LLC
New York, NY

Mallarmé, Stéphane
    *The Anchor Anthology of French Poetry from Nerval to Valery*
    "The Pristine, The Perennial, and the Beauteous Today…"
    Edited by Angel Flores, translated by Katie Flores
    Copyright © 1958 and renewed 1986
    Used with permission of Anchor Books, a division of Random House Inc.
    New York, NY
Yeats, W. B.
    *The Collected Works of W.B. Yeats,*
    *Volume I: The Poems, Revised*, edited by Richard J. Finneran
    "Leda and the Swan"
    The Macmillan Company (1928)
    Copyright renewed © 1956 by Georgie Yeats
    Reprinted with the permission of
    Scribner Division of Simon & Schuster, Inc.  1996
    New York, NY
Horan, Robert
    *The Yale Younger Poets Anthology*
    "Soft Swimmer, Winter Swan" (1948)
    Ed. George Bradley
    Yale University Press, 1998
    New Haven, CT
Sarton, May
    *The Silence Now and New and Uncollected Earlier Poems*
    "Blizzard"
    Copyright © 1988
    W. W. Norton & Company
    New York, NY
Larkin, Philip
    *Collected Poems*
    "Blizzard"
    Copyright © 1988, 1989 by the estate of Philip Larkin
    Reprinted by permission of Farrar, Straus, Giroux, LLC
    New York, NY
Larkin, Philip
    *Collected Poems*
    "Winter"
    Copyright © 1988, 1989 by the estate of Philip Larkin
    Reprinted by permission of Farrar, Straus, Giroux, LLC
    New York, NY

Dickey, James
    *Poems (1957 – 1967)*
    "Fog Envelopes the Animals"
    Copyright © 1967 by James Dickey
    Reprinted by permission of Wesleyan University Press
    Middletown, CT
Jeffers, Robinson
    *The Collected Poetry of Robinson Jeffers*
    "Flight of Swan"
    Edited by Tim Hunt, Volume 2, 1928 - 1938
    Copyright © 1938, 1966 renewed by Donnan and Garth Jeffers
    Used with permission of Stanford University Press
    Stanford, CA
MacEwen, Gwendolyn
    *Afterworlds*
    "The Death of the Loch Ness Monster"
    Celebrate the Fourth International Festival of
    Authors at Harbourfront (Toronto) in 1983
    Published in 1987 by McClelland & Stewart
    Toronto, Canada
Lawrence, D. H.
    *The Plumed Serpent*
    "The Living Quetzalcoatl", Pg 343
    Copyright © 1926 by Alfred A. Knopf,
    Division of Random House Inc.
    And renewed 1954 by Frieda Lawrence Ravagli.
    Used by permission of Alfred A. Knopf, a division of Random House Inc.
    New York, NY
Meredith, William
    *Effort at Speech: New and Selected Poems*
    "Orpheus"
    Copyright © 1997 by William Meredith
    Tri Quarterly Books/Northwestern University Press
    All rights reserved; used by permission of Northwestern University Press
    and the author.
    Evanston, IL
Vinal, Harold
    *The Yale Younger Poets Anthology*
    "To Persephone" (1922)
    Edited by George Bradley
    Yale University Press, 1998
    New Haven, CT

Roethke, Theodore
  *The Collected Poems of Theodore Roethke*
  "The Swan" (1958)
  Reprinted by permission of Doubleday,
  a Division of Random House Inc. 1975
  New York, NY
Plath, Sylvia
  *The Collected Poems*
  "Winter Landscape, with Rooks"
  Copyright © 1965, 1981 Estate of Sylvia Plath
  Edited by Ted Hughes
  Used with permission of HarperPerennial
  a divison of  HarperCollins Publishers
  New York, NY
 H.D. (Doolittle, Hilda)
  *Collected Poems 1912 – 1944*
  "Birds in Snow"
  Copyright © 1982 by the Estate of Hilda Doolittle
  Reprinted by permission of New Directions Publishing Corp.
  New York, NY

# SPRING

Thomas, Dylan
  *The Poems of Dylan Thomas*
  "The Force that Through the Green Fuse Drives The Flower"
  Copyright © 1939 by New Directions Publishing Corp.
  Reprinted by Permission of New Directions Publishing Corp.
  New York, NY
Chaucer, Geoffrey
  *The Canterbury Tales*
  "The Prologe"
  Edited by A. Kent Hieatt and Constance Hieatt
  A Bantam Classic, 1954
  New York, NY
Eliot, T.S.
  *Collected Poems 1909 - 1962*
  "The Waste Land, I. The Burial of the Dead"
  Verse 1 – 18
  Harcourt Brace Jovanovich Publishers 1934
  Orlando, FL

Fallon, Peter
  *Contemporary Irish Poetry: An Anthology*
  "Spring Song"
  Ed. Anthony Bradley
  New and revised edition
  Copyright © 1988
  The Regents of the University of California Press
  Berkeley, CA
Barber, Theodore Xenophon
  *The Human Nature of Birds*
  "Flexible Territoriality"
  Copyright ©1993
  Penguin Book USA, Inc.
  New York, NY
Spenser, Edmund
  *The New Oxford Book of Sixteenth Century Verse*
  "Prothalamion" Verse 37 -54
  Edited by Emrys Jones
  Oxford University Press, 1991
  Oxford, UK
Porter, Anne
  *An Altogether Different Language:  Poems 1934 – 1994*
  "An Easter Lily"
  Zoland Books, 1994
  Cambridge, MA
White, E.B.
  *The Trumpet of the Swan*
  "A Visitor" Pg 23
  Illustrated by Edward Frascino
  Used with permission by HarperCollins Publishers 1970
  New York, NY
Moore,  Marianne
  *The Complete Poems of Marianne Moore*
  "No Swan So Fine"
  Copyright © 1935
  Copyright renewed © 1963 by Marianne Moore and T.S. Eliot
  Reprinted with the permission of Scribner,
  Imprint of Simon & Schuster Adult Publishing Group
  New York, NY

Kunitz, Stanley
    *The Collected Poems*
    "When The Light Falls"
    Copyright © 2000 by Stanley Kunitz
    Used with permission of W. W. Norton and Company, Inc.
    New York, NY
Coatsworth, Elizabeth
    *Poems (1957)*
    "The Swan"
    Reprinted by Permission of Paterson Marsh Ltd.
    Little Wick, UK
Shakespeare, William
    *King John, Act V, Scene VII 4-50*
    "Cygnet to this pale faint swan"
    *The Edition of the Shakespeare Head Press, Oxford*
    Barnes and Noble, Inc. (1994)
    New York, NY
Lorenz, Konrad Z.
    *King Solomon's Ring (1952)*
    "The Perennial Retainers"
    Translated from the German by Marjorie Kerr Wilson
    Copyright © 1952 by Harper & Row
    Used with permission of HarperCollins Publishers
    London, UK
The Holy Bible
    *King James Version*
    The Song of Solomon
    Chapter 2: 1 – 13
    Thomas Nelson Publishers 1994
    Nashville, TN
Longley, Michael
    *Selected Poems*
    "Swans Mating"
    Copyright © 1999
    Used with permission of Wake Forest University Press
    Winston-Salem, NC
Clief – Stefanon, Lyrae Van
    *Black Swan*
    "Black Swan"
    Copyright © 2002
    Reprinted by permission of University of Pittsburgh Press
    Pittsburgh, PA

Wilbur, Richard
    *Walking to Sleep: New Poems and Translations*
    "Under Cygnus"
    Copyright © 1966 by Richard Wilbur
    Reprinted by permission of Harcourt, Inc.
    Orlando, Florida
The Holy Bible
    *King James Version*
    "Leviathan" (Isaiah 27:1, Psalm 104:26, Job 41:1-2)
    Thomas Nelson Publishers, 1994
    Nashville, TN

## SUMMER

Thomas, Dylan
    *Collected Poems 1934 – 1952*
    "Fern Hill"
    Copyright © 1957 by the Trustees for the Copyright of Dylan Thomas
    A New Directions Book
    New York, NY
Neruda, Pablo
    *Extravagaria*
    "Pastoral"
    Translated by Alastair Reid
    Translation copyright © 1974
    Reprinted by permission of Farrar, Straus, and Giroux, LLC
    New York, NY
Dickinson, Emily
    "Hope Is The Thing With Feathers"
    Reprinted by permission of the publishers and the Trustees of
    Amherst College from *The Poems of Emily Dickinson*
    Thomas H. Johnson, ed.
    The Belknap Press of Harvard University Press, Copyright ©
    1951, 1955, 1979, 1883 by the President and Fellows of Harvard College.
    Cambridge, Mass
Tennyson, Alfred Lord
    *A Collection of Poems*
    "The Dragonfly" from The Two Voices 1833
    Selected and with an Introduction by Christopher Ricks 1972
    Used with permission of Doubleday Division of Random House Inc.
    Garden City, NY

Merrill, James
  *Collected Poems*
  "To A Butterfly"
  From *Collected Poems* by James Merrill, edited by J.D. McClatchy and
  Stephen Yenser, copyright © 2001 by the Literary Estate of
  James Merrill at Washington University. Used by permission of Alfred
  A. Knopf, a division of Random House, Inc.
  New York, NY
Merrill, James
  *Collected Poems*
  "The Black Swan"
  From *Collected Poems* by James Merrill, edited by J.D. McClatchy and
  Stephen Yenser, , copyright © 2001 by the Literary Estate of
  James Merrill at Washington University. Used by permission of
  Alfred A. Knopf, a division of Random House, Inc.
  New York, NY
Apollinaire, Guillaume
  *The Anchor Anthology of French Poetry from Nerval to Valery*
  "Dusk"
  Edited by Angel Flores, Translated by Dudley Fitts
  Copyright © 1958 and renewed 1986
  Used with permission of Anchor Books, a division of Random House Inc.
  New York, NY
Gershwin, George;  Gershwin, Ira;  Heyward, Dubose and Dorothy
  *Summertime (From "Porgy and Bess")*
  © Copyright 1935 ( Renewed) George Gershwin Music, Ira Gershwin  music,
  DuBose and Dorothy Heyward Memorial fund Publishing (ASCAP)
  All rights Administered WB Music Corp. (ASCAP)
  All rights reserved                              Used by permission
  Warner Bros. Publications U.S. Inc.,
  Miami, FL
McNeill, Louise
  *Hill Daughter: New and Selected Poems (1991)*
  "Memoria"
  Reprinted by permission of the University of Pittsburgh Press
  Copyright © 1991
  Pittsburgh, PA
Niklander, Hannu
  *Nicely Curtsying Daughter*
  "The  Swan"
  Copyright © 1983
  Fagerkulla 75
  Finland

Nash, Ogden
  *The New Yorker 1950*
  "The Swan"
  Curtis Brown, LTD
  New York, NY
Bly, Robert
  *The Kabir Book*
  "The Swan"
  Copyright © 1971, 1977 by Robert Bly
  ©1977 by the Seventies Press
  Reprinted by permission of Beacon Press
  Boston, MA
Rilke, Rainer Maria
  *Selected Poems*
  "The Swan"
  Copyright © 1908
  Translated by Albert Ernest Fleming Copyright © 1983, 1985
  Reproduced by permission of Routledge/Taylor & Francis Books, Inc.
  New York, NY
Lawrence, D. H.
  *The Complete Poems of D. H. Lawrence*
  "Leda"
  Edited by V. de Sola Pinto & F. W. Roberts, Copyright © 1964,
  1971, by Angelo Ravagli and C. M. Weekly, Executors of the Estate of
  Frieda Lawrence Ravagli. Used by permission of Viking Penguin,
  a division of Penguin Group (USA) Inc.
  New York, NY
Anderson, Maggie
  *A Space Filled With Moving*
  "Summer Solstice"
  Copyright © 1992
  Reprinted by permission of the University of Pittsburgh Press
  Pittsburgh, PA
Coleridge, Samuel Taylor
  *Untune The Sky: Poems Of Music And The Dance*
  "The Desired Swan-Song", Helen Plotz (Comp)
  Crowell 1957
  New York, NY
Baudelaire, Charles
  *Halfway Down the Hall, New and Selected Poems*
  "The  Swan"
  Translated by Rachel Hadas
  Copyright © 1998
  Reprinted by permission of Wesleyan University Press
  Middletown, CT

Lawrence, D. H.
    *The Complete Poems of D. H. Lawrence*
    "Swan"
    Edited by V. de Sola Pinto & F. W. Roberts, copyright © 1964,
    1971, by Angelo Ravagli and C. M. Weekly, Executors of the Estate of
    Frieda Lawrence Ravagli. Used by permission of Viking Penguin,
    a division of Penguin Group (USA) Inc.
    New York, NY
Lucie-Smith, Edward
    *Voices in the Gallery*
    Part V, Bellissima!
    "Blue" pg. 194
    Copyright © 1986
    Tate Gallery Publications
    London, UK

## FALL

Auden, Wystan Hugh
    *On This Island*
    "Now The Leaves Are Falling Fast"
    Copyright © 1937
    Random House, Inc.
    Used by permission of Random House, Inc.
    New York, NY
Succop, Margaret Phillips
    *Climb to the Stars*
    "Autumn Leaves"
    Dorrance & Company 1952
    Philadelphia, Pa.
Hopkins, Gerard Manley 1918
    *The Poems of Gerard Manley Hopkins by Hopkins*
    "Spring and Fall"
    Oxford University Press Copyright 1970
    Oxford, UK
James Merrill
    *Collected Poems*
    "Thistledown"
    From *Collected Poems* by James Merrill, edited by J.D. McClatchy and
    Stephen Yenser, copyright © 2001 by the Literary Estate of
    James Merrill at Washington University. Used by permission of Alfred
    A. Knopf, a division of Random House, Inc.
    New York, NY

Zabel, Morton Dauwen
    *Poetry*
    "Hoar Frost"
    The Estate of Morton Dauwen Zabel Copyright © 1928
    Dr. Matthew A. Sutton
    Chicago, IL
Merwin, W. S.
    *Flower and Hand: Poems 1977– 1983*
    "Autumn Evening"
    Copyright © 1977 by W.S. Merwin
    Reprinted with the permission of the Wylie Agency Inc.
    New York, NY
Hölderlin Friedrich
    *Hymns and Fragment*
    "Half of Life"
    Translated and introduced Richard Sieburth
    Copyright © 1984
    Princeton University Press
    Published with the Permission of Princeton University Press
    Princeton, NJ
MacLeish, Archibald
    *Collected Poems (1917– 1982)*
    "Immortal Autumn"
    Copyright © 1985 by The Estate of Archibald MacLeish.
    Reprinted by permission of the Houghton Mifflin Company.
    All rights reserved.
    New York, NY
Carruth, Hayden
    *Collected Shorter Poems, 1946– 1991*
    "The Wild Swans at Norfolk"
    Copyright © 1992
    Copper Canyon Press
    Port Townsend, WA
Tennyson, Alfred Lord
    *A Collection of Poems*
    "The Dying Swan"
    Selected and with an Introduction by Christopher Ricks 1972
    Used with permission of Doubleday Division of Random House Inc.
    Garden City, NY

Bierlein, J. F.
*Parallel Myths*
"Angus Og"
Copyright © 1994 by J.F. Bierlein.
Used by permission of Ballantine Books,
a division of Random House, Inc.
New York, NY

Gibbons, Orlando
*The First Set of Madrigals and Mottet of 5*
"The Silver Swanne"
Copyright © 1612
Appointed Organist at Westminster Abbey 1622
London, UK

Aesop Fables
"The Swan and Goose"
Translated by William Ellery Leonard
Crowell Inc (1957)
New York, NY

Yeats, W. B.
*The Collected Works of W.B. Yeats,*
*Volume I: The Poems, Revised*, edited by Richard J. Finneran
"The Wild Swans at Coole"
The Macmillan Company (1928)
Copyright renewed © 1956 by Georgie Yeats
Reprinted with the permission of
Scribner Division of Simon & Schuster, Inc. 1996
New York, NY

Baring-Gould, Sabine
*Myths of the Middle Ages*
"Swan-Maidens", pg 120
Irish Melodies, No. ii 9; Thomas Moore (1807)
Edited by John Matthews
Blandford, A Cassell Imprint 1996
London, UK

Frazer, Sir James George
*The Golden Bough: A Study in Magic And Religion*
"The External Soul in Folk-Tales" Chapter 66
Copyright © 1922 by The Macmillan Company;
Copyright © 1950 by Barclays Bank Ltd.
Reprinted with the permission of Scribner,
Imprint of Simon & Schuster Adult Publishing Group
New York, NY

Helprin, Mark
*Swan Lake*
"Pg 48 lines 6 -12"
Ariel Books
Fairfield, CT

Baring-Gould, Sabine
*Myths of the Middle Ages*
"Swan-Maidens, Pg 116
Edited by John Matthews
Blandford, A Cassell Imprint 1996
London, U.K.

Guerber, H.A.
*Myths Of The Norsemen: From the Eddas and Sagas*
"Wayland and the Valkyrs"
Translated Thorpe, "Lay of Volsung"
Unabridged republication by George G. Harrap & Company, London, 1909
Re-edition Dover Edition, 1992
Mineola, New York

Eschenbach, Wolfram Von
*Parzival*
Translated by A. T. Hatto 1980
Reproduced by permission of Penquin Books Ltd.
London, UK

Southey, Robert
*Poems of Robert Southey: Ballads and Metrical Tales*
"Rudiger"
[The story has been adapted from Thomas Heywood 1797]
Edited by Maurice H. Fitzgerald, M.A.
Henry Frowe
Oxford University Press 1909
London, UK

Lindsay, Vachel
*Johnny Appleseed and Other Poems*
"On The Garden Wall"
Copyright © 1913, 1914, 1917
Macmillan Publishing
New York, NY

Poe, Edgar Allan
*Tamerlane and Other Poems*
"Fanny"
Copyright 1827
Calvin F.S. Thomas, Printer
Boston, MA

Meredith, William
    *Effort At Speech*
    "Poem"
    Copyright © 1997 by William Meredith
    Tri Quarterly Books/Northwestern University Press
    All rights reserved; used by permission of Northwestern University Press
    and the author.
    Evanston, IL
Oliver, Mary
    *No Voyage and Other Poems*
    "Swans on the River Ayr"
    Copyright © 1963, 1993 by Mary Oliver
    Used by permission of the Molly Malone Cook Literary Agency
    Provincetown, MA
Hollander, John
    *Types of Shape*
    "Swan and Shadow"
    Yale University Press 1991
    New Haven, CT

## EPILOGUE

Rexroth, Kenneth
    *The Selected Longer Poems*
    "The Silver Swan II"
    Copyright © 1967 by Kenneth Rexroth
    Reprinted by permission of New Directions Publishing Corp.
    New York, NY

## PARTIAL SOURCES

Romer, Alfred Sherwood
    *The Vertebrate Body,* Figure 58,59
    Copyright © 1949
    W.B. Saunders Company
    Philadelphia, PA
Johnsgard, Paul A.
    *Ducks, Geese and Swans of the World*
    Copyright © 1978
    University of Nebraska Press
    Lincoln, NE

Stivens, Dal
    *The Incredible Egg*
    Copyright © 1974
    Webright and Talley
    New York, NY
Prum, Richard O.; Brush, Alan H.
    *Which Came First, The Feather or the Bird?*
    Scientific American
    Volume 288, Number 3
    Copyright © March 2003
Ehrlich, Paul R.; Dobkin, David S.; Wheye, Darryl
    *The Birder's Handbook*
    Copyright © 1988
    Published by Simon and Schuster, and Fireside, Inc.
    New York, NY
Leahy, Christopher
    *The Birdwatcher's Companion*
    Copyright © 1982
    Random House Value Publishing, Inc. 1997
    New York, NY
Hornblower, Simon and Spawforth, Anthony (Edited by)
    *The Oxford Classical Dictionary*
    Third Edition Revised Published 2003
    Copyright © 1949, 1970, 1996, 2003
    Oxford University Press
    Oxford, UK
Quammen, David
    *The Song of the Dodo, Island Biogeography In An Age of Extinctions*
    Copyright © 1996
    Scribner
    New York, NY
Lieberman, Bruce S.
    *Paleobiogeography*
    Copyright © 2000
    Kluwer Academic / Plenum Publishers
    New York, NY
Thoms, William J.
    *Early English Prose Romances, with Bibliographical and Historical and*
    *Introductions. Volume III, Helyas*
    "Helias, Knight of the Swan"
    Second Edition, Enlarged. 1858
    Nattali and Bond, Publishers
    London, U.K.

# GLOSSARY

**Avifauna**

Cob - An adult male swan; refers to the "Crown", i.e., to the fleshy enlarged knob above the bill and the nostril.

Cygnet - A young swan

Pen - An adult female swan; refers to the 12th century Vulgate Latin a "penna", (plumes, feathers, pinions, or wings). The 14th century reflects the special use of quills in writing.

**Botany**

Algae - A group of chiefly aquatic, nonvascular plants with colors of green, yellow, brown, and red. The Families include Chlorophyla and Enteromorpha.

Bull Thistle - Thistle is the name given to a group of plants characterized by spines and prickles. Thistles belong to the Family Compositae. The common Bull Thistle is a beautiful purple flower often seen in fields and pastures. The important genera is *Cirsium* with species *lanceolatum* and *vulgare.*

Bulrush - Tall rushes or sedges growing in wetlands. The Family is Cyperaceae, and the botanical term is *Scirpus lacustris.*

Cattails - Tall reedy marsh plants with brown furry fruiting spikes. The Family is Typhaceae and the genus is *Typha,* known in the vernacular as Reed-Mace.

Chicken Mushroom - Yellow variety; a polypore consisting of a flat, fan-shaped, bright yellow fungi. The tiny pores are too small to see without magnification. The caps, 2 to 12 inches across, have yellow flesh that looks like chicken meat.

Duckweeds - The Family Lemnaceae, a small floating aquatic monocotyledonous plant. The genus is *Lemna.*

Muskgrass - The Family Characeae of freshwater green algae, of the genus *Chara,* resembling horsetails and encrusted with calcareous deposits. The vernacular is the stonewort.

Nest - Black Australian and mute swans build a nest surrounded by water, marsh, or emergent shore. Herbaceous vegetation of reeds, bark, leaves, cattails, sticks, muskgrass, wild celery, etc. to form a mound. Often the nest is built on the previous site. Occasionally, old muskrat houses are the beginning of a new nest. The nest is approximately eight feet in diameter and two feet above the water. Both sexes build on the site; 80% of the nest is formed by the pen. Eggs are deposited every 48 hours until the clutch (usually 6-7) is laid. The pen incubates the eggs from 35-38 days. The cob during this incubation period becomes increasingly territorial.

| | |
|---|---|
| Pondweeds - | The Family Zannichelliaceae, the genus *Potamogeton*, of aquatic plants with jointed usual root stems, spikes of greenish flowers, and submerged leaves. |
| Water lily - | The Family Nymphaeaceae of aquatic plants, with floating leaves and bright flowers. |

## Cladistics

| | |
|---|---|
| Anseriformes - | The order of birds including screamers, ducks, geese, and swans. |
| Anatidae - | The family of birds including ducks, geese, and swans. |
| Genus - | Swans |
| Species - | Mute and Black Australian swans |

## Ethology

| | |
|---|---|
| Brooding - | Collectively the young hatched from a single clutch of eggs.  Black Australian swans double-brood in the winter and spring. |
| Clutch - | The complete number of eggs laid by a single female incubated simultaneously. |
| Eggs - | Birds developed about 150 million years ago during the Jurassic period when reptiles were reaching their peak.  In a famous lecture in 1868 Thomas Huxley (1825-1895) showed that *Archaeopteryx lithographica* was "descent with modification" made flesh, a bird transforming its reptilian origins.  The cleidoic (closed) eggs are virtually self-contained life-support systems.  The egg shell contains germ cells, spermatozoon, a yolk, glycoprotein, the shell-gland of matrix of fibrous protein, calcium carbonate crystal, an insoluble uric acid.  The embryo and the yolk are protected by two membranes, the amnion and the chorion.  The shell provides calcium pores allowing an equilibrium between oxygen and carbon dioxide. |
| Egg tooth - | A small calcareous tip of the bill which develops in birds and reptiles to break through the eggshell when hatching. |
| Fledgling period - | The period between hatching and initial flight in birds. |
| Immature birds - | The age class in birds that follows the juvenile period but precedes sexual maturity.  This distinct subadult plumage and behavior require 1-2 years.  Mating occurs after the third year. |
| Incubation - | The application of heat to an egg by an adult bird (104° F). The gestation period is the period between the incubation to hatching.  The incubation period of mute and black Australian swans is  34-38 days. |
| Moult - | Postnuptial breeding season when the plumage is lost and flight feathers are regrown. |

| Precocial species - | Hatched with eyes open, covered with down, and leaving the nest within 1-2 days (cygnets). In contrast, the altricial birds are hatched with eyes closed, with little or no down, incapable of departing from the nest, and fed by the parents. (All songbirds are altricial). The cygnets' in-egg development contains almost twice the calories per unit weight as songbirds. |
|---|---|
| Swan-song - | A plaintive threnody secondary to the dying of a mate or the loss of cygnets. (The female Black Australian swan swims around the lake for 2-3 days after the loss of her cygnet.) |
| Swan-sounds - | The swan's windpipe has a distinguished vocal structure (Syrinx) distal to the glottis. Depending on its mood, the swan may hiss, snort, bugle, cry or be mute. |

## Mythopoeia

| Cycnus - | The mythical name of four young men changed into swans: 1. The son of Apollo. 2. Achilles killed by a trojan at Troy. 3. The King of Ligurian's was a lover to Phaëthon; he is placed among the stars as the constellation Cygnus. 4. A son of Ares is killed by Hercules. |
|---|---|
| Cygnus - | The Latin and Greek mythology show the northern constellation near the vernal equinoctical point. The Swan lies between Lyra and Pegasus in The Milky Way. |
| Gemini - | Two stars, the twins; Castor and Pollux. |
| Leda - | The wife of King Tyndareus of Sparta; Leda bore two mortal children to him, Castor and Clytemnesta (Agamenon's wife). Zeus, in the form of a swan copulated with Leda, who subsequently produced an egg containing Helen and the Dioscouri (Castor and immortal Pollux). This is the beginning of the Judgement of Paris, a thousand ships, Helen's betrayal of Ilium, and the immortal poem of the Iliad. |
| Helias - | The History of Helias Knight of the Swan as related in the following pages is an old English version of a very early and very popular romance. It is supposed by Sir Francis Palgrave that the most ancient form in which the story exists is in the *Chronicle of Tongres* by the *Maitre de Guise* much of which was afterwards incorporated into the *Mer des Hystoires*, William J. Thoms, F.S.A. There is also an Icelandic Saga of Helis the Knight of the Swan in which he is represented as a Son of Julius Caesar; and a similar legend is introduced into the German Romance of Lohengrin of which an edition was printed at Heidelberg so late as 1813. The tradition that the celebrated Godfrey of Boulogne was lineally descended from the Knight of the Swan is still current in the Duchy of Cleves, and forms one of the most interesting stories in Otmar's *Volksagen*. It must have obtained an early and general circulation in Flanders; for Nicolaes de Klerc who wrote at the commencement of the 14th century (1318) thus refers to it in his *Brabandshe Yeesten*....because formerly the Dukes of Brabant have been much belied, to wit, *that they came with a Swan*, I have undertaken to disclose the truth, and to propound it in Dutch Rhyme....From these concurrent sources it seems probable that the original fable was fabricated in Belgium or at least on the borders of the Rhine and a further evidence of the correctness of such a supposition is to be found in the circumstances of the Legend forming the subject of a Flemish chap-book of frequent occurrence at the present day. |

# Appendix

---

## Comparison of Mute and Black Swans

| | **Mute** | **Black** |
|---|---|---|
| **I. Cladistics** | | |
| Order | Anseriformes | Anseriformes |
| Family | Anatidae | Anatidae |
| Genus | *Cygnus* | *Cygnus* |
| Species | olor | atratus |

**II. Geography**

a. **Indigenous**

1. Breeding: British Isles, North Central Europe Steppes of Asia, Siberia and Mongolia — Australia and the North of Tasmania

2. Wintering: North Africa, Near East, Northwest India and Korea — Australia and the North of Tasmania

b. **Introduction**

1. North America, Australia, South Africa, China, and New Zealand — North America, China, New Zealand

**III. Natural History**

a. **Anatomical:**

| Mute | Black |
|---|---|
| Length 55-63 Inches | 38-46 Inches |
| Wingspan 70-80 Inches | 55-72 Inches |
| Weight 22-26 Pounds | 12-14 Pounds |

b. **Breeding:**

1. Sexual Maturity: 3 years — 3-4 years
2. Breeding: March to June — The Black Australian Swan several clutches with 2-3 eggs in winter, with a second clutch of 5-8 eggs at the last week of May

3. Number of clutches:  1                Number of clutches:  1-2
4. Clutch:  5-8 eggs                  Winter 2-3, Spring 5-7 eggs
5. Incubation: 35-38 days            35-38 days
6. Fledgling period:   3-4 months      3-4 months

c. **Ethology:**

1. The alpha male tends to be very territorial and aggressive throughout the year.  The pen is less territorial after the cygnets are fledglings.

   The Black Australian swans are more sociable than the mutes.

2. Domestic mates tend to have very strong pair bonding.

   Domestic mates tend to have strong pair bonding.

3. Language: Hissing and snort (The pen loses her cygnet and grieves for 2-3 days.)

   Hissing, snort, plaintive dirge

4. Foraging by upending in water

   Foraging by upending in water

d. **Lifespan:**

1. 50 years                            20 years

## IV.  Semiferal or Domestic

1. Temperate zone with marshes, slow rivers and lakes
2. Herbaceous pondweeds, muskgrass, duckweed, green algae and terrestrial grasses
3. Protein grain supplements during fall and winter
4. Semiferal and domestic swans winter around powerplants, submerged pumps or aerolators.

# Index

Aesop:  The Swan and Goose, pg 162.
Anderson, Maggie:  Summer Solstice, pg 134.
Apollinaire, Guillaume:  Dusk, pg 124.
Auden, Wystan Hugh:  Now the Leaves are Falling Fast, pg 144.

Barber, Theodore Xenophon:  Flexible Territoriality, pg 64.
Baring-Gould, Sabine:  The song of Fionnala, pg 166;
    The Swan-Maiden, pg 172.
Baudelaire, Charles:  The Swan, pg 136.
Bierlein, J.F.:  Angus Og, pg 160.
Bible, The Holy:  Leviathan (Isaiah 27:1, Psalm 104:26,
    Job 41:1-2), pg 106; The Song of Solomon, Chapter 2: 1-13,
    pg 92.
Bly, Robert:  The Swan, pg 130.
Bogan, Louise:  Winter Swan, pg 14.

Carruth, Hayden:  The Wild Swans at Norfolk, pg 156.
Chaucer, Geoffrey:  The Canterbury Tales, pg 60.
Clief-Stefanon, Lyrae Van:  Leda, pg 10; Black Swan pg 96.
Coatsworth, Elizabeth:  The Swan, pg 88.
Coleridge, Samuel Taylor:  The Desired Swan-Song, pg 138.

Dickey, James:  Fog Envelopes the Animals, pg 38.
Dickinson, Emily:  "Hope" is the Thing with Feathers, pg 114.
Doolittle, Hilda (H.D.):  Birds in Snow, pg 54.

Eliot, T.S.:  Little Gidding, pg 16; The Waste Land, pg 60.
Emerson, Ralph Waldo:  The Snowstorm, pg 6.
Eschenbach, Wolfram Von:  Parzival, pg 176.

Fallon, Peter:  Spring Song, pg 62.
Frazer, Sir James George:  The External Soul in Folk-Tales, pg 168.

Gershwin, George; Gershwin, Ira; Heyward, Dubose and
    Dorothy:  Summertime from "Porgy and Bess" pg 126.
Gibbons, Orlando:  The Silver Swan, pg 162.
Guerber, H.A.:  The Wayland and the Valkyrs, pg 174.

Helprin, Mark:  Odette, pg 170.
Hölderlin, Friedrich:  Half of Life, pg 153.

Hollander, John:  Metathalamia, pg 18; Swan and Shadow,
    pg 186.
Hopkins, Gerard Manley:  Spring and Fall:  To a Young Child,
    pg 147.
Horan, Robert:  Soft Swimmer, Winter Swan, pg 28.

Jarrell, Randall:  The Black Swan, pg 20.
Jeffers, Robinson:  Flight of Swans, pg 40.

Kunitz, Stanley:  When the Light Falls, pg 84.

Larkin, Philip:  Blizzard, pg 30; Winter, pg 36.
Lawrence, D.H.:  The Living Quetzalcoatl, pg 44; Leda, pg 132;
    Swan, pg 139.
Lindsay, Vachel:  On the Garden Wall, pg 180.
Longley, Michael:  Swans Mating, pg 94.
Lorenz, Konrad Z.:  The Perennial Retainers, pg 90.
Lucie-Smith, Edward:  Blue, pg 140.

MacEwen, Gwendolyn:  The Death of the Loch Ness Monster,
    pg 42.
MacLeish, Archibald:  Immortal Autumn, pg 154.
Mallarmé, Stéphane:  The Pristine, the Perennial, and the
    Beauteous Today…, pg 25.
McNeill, Louise:  Memoria, pg 127.
Meredith, William:  Orpheus, pg 46; Poem, pg 182.
Merrill, James:  To a Butterfly, pg 116; The Black Swan, pg 118,
    Thistledown, pg 148.
Merwin, W.S.:  Autumn Evening, Pg 152.
Moore, Marianne:  No Swan So Fine, pg 83.

Nash, Odgen:  The Swan, pg 129.
Nathan, Leonard:  Dairy of a Left-Handed Birdwatcher, prologue.
Neruda, Pablo:  Pastoral, pg 112.
Niklander, Hannu:  The Swan, pg 128.

Oliver, Mary:  Swans on the River Ayr, pg 184.

Plath, Sylvia:  Winter Landscape, With Rooks, pg 52.
Poe, Edgar Allan:  Fanny, pg 181.
Porter, Anne:  An Easter Lily, pg 68.

Rexroth, Kenneth:  Leda Hidden, pg 2; Epilogue; The Silver
    Swan, pg 188.
Rilke, Rainer Maria:  Leda, pg 12; The Swan, pg 132.
Roethke, Theodore:  The Swan, pg 50.

Sarton, May:  Blizzard, pg 30.
Shakespeare, William:  Cygnet to this pale faint swan, pg 89.
Southey, Robert:  Rudiger, pg 178.
Spenser, Edmund:  Prothalamion, pg 66.
Succop, Margaret Phillips:  A Winter Day, pg 8; Autumn Leaves,
    pg 146.

Tennyson, Alfred Lord:  Dragonfly, pg 115; The Dying Swan,
    pg 158.

Thomas, Dylan:  The Force That Through The Green Fuse Drives
    The Flower, pg 58; Fern Hill, pg 110.

Vinal, Harold:  To Persephone, pg 48.

White, E.B.:  An Egg....., pg 69.
Wilbur, Richard:  Years End, pg 4; Under Cygnus, pg 100.
Wylie, Elinor:  Velvet Shoes, pg 9.

Yeats, W.B.:  Leda and the Swan, pg 26; The Wild Swans at Coole,
    pg 164.

Zabel, Morton Dauwen:  Hoar Frost, pg 150.